Meet the staff of
THE TREEHOUSE TIMES

AMY—The neighborhood newspaper is Amy's most brilliant idea ever—a perfect project for her and her friends, with a perfect office location—the treehouse in Amy's backyard!

ERIN—A great athlete despite her tiny size, Erin will be a natural when it comes to covering any sports-related story in the town of Kirkridge.

LEAH—Tall and thin with long, dark hair and blue eyes, Leah is the artistic-type. She hates drawing attention to herself, but with her fashion-model looks, it's impossible not to.

ROBIN—With her bright red hair, freckles and green eyes, and a loud chirpy voice, nobody can miss Robin—and Robin misses nothing when it comes to getting a good story.

Keep Your Nose in the News with
THE TREEHOUSE TIMES Series
by Page McBrier

(#2) THE KICKBALL CRISIS

Coming Soon

(#3) SPAGHETTI BREATH

PAGE McBRIER grew up in Indianapolis, Indiana, and St. Louis, Missouri, in a large family with lots of pets. In college she studied children's theater and later taught drama in California and New York. She currently lives in Rowayton, Connecticut, with her husband, Peter Morrison, a film producer, and their two small sons.

THE TREEHOUSE TIMES #1

Under 12 Not Allowed

Page McBrier

AN AVON CAMELOT BOOK

THE TREEHOUSE TIMES #1: UNDER 12 NOT ALLOWED is an original publication of Avon Books. This work has never before appeared in book form.

AVON BOOKS
A division of
The Hearst Corporation
105 Madison Avenue
New York, New York 10016

First Avon Camelot Printing: October 1989

CAMELOT TRADEMARK REG. U.S. PAT. OFF. AND IN OTHER COUNTRIES, MARCA REGISTRADA, HECHO EN U.S.A.

Printed in the U.S.A.

OPM 10 9 8 7 6 5 4 3 2 1

To my husband, Peter

Chapter One

"One, two, three, LIFT!" Grunting in unison, Amy Evans and her friend Robin Ryan braced their bodies against the end of the old wooden sofa frame and lifted it slowly toward the hole in the treehouse floor.

"Here it comes!" they heard Erin Valdez yell at the other end. "Don't drop it."

Robin rolled her eyes at Amy and hooted. "Are you kidding me?" she shouted up. "If we drop it we'll be killed instantly."

Above them, Erin and Leah Fox started to giggle. "Don't make us laugh, Robin," Leah called down. "It wastes too much energy."

Robin snorted and wiped her forehead on her blouse. "Whoever heard of a treehouse with a sofa in it anyway?"

1

Amy grinned, her body staggering under the weight of the sofa. "Just push, would you?"

"Aaargh!" Robin groaned, pushing up. Slowly, the couch tilted forward.

"You almost have it," Erin shouted from above. "One more push."

Amy squinted her eyes and concentrated. Next to her, Robin looked like she was about to pop a blood vessel.

Boom! With a loud thud, the couch crashed onto the treehouse floor.

"We did it!" yelled Erin. "And it's still in one piece!"

"Hooray!" shouted Amy as she hurried toward the ladder. "Come on, Robin. Let's go see what it looks like."

Upstairs, Erin and Leah had already piled the cushions back on the sofa, where they had collapsed and were fanning themselves with old magazines.

"Whew," said Robin, plopping down beside them. "Do you think Ms. Willis will excuse me from P.E. for this?"

Amy circled the room, too excited to pay attention. "It looks great up here now," she said. "Just like a real office." She pointed to the corner. "A card table, a typewriter, office supplies . . ." She stopped. "Hey, I've got a good idea. Why don't I get my pig calendar

2

from my room and put it over the desk? We can use it to keep track of our deadlines."

From her position on the couch, Erin solemnly raised her hand. "To the *Treehouse Times*," she said. "The best neighborhood newspaper Kirkridge will ever have!"

"Hip, hip, hooray," chorused everyone else.

Amy pushed her bangs off her glasses and grinned at her friends. She was famous for coming up with projects, but starting a neighborhood newspaper was probably her best idea yet. She'd come up with it a few weeks ago after her sixth grade class did a newspaper unit in school and toured the offices of the *St. Louis Post-Dispatch*. "It'll be fun," she'd told her friends Leah, Erin, and Robin when she'd asked them to help her. "We can report on any news around the neighborhood *and* it'll give us something exciting to do."

Amy hated to sit around, but more important than that she really liked finding out about people. Her brother, Patrick, said she was nosey, but that really wasn't it. A newspaper was a great way to bring people together.

Amy watched Erin and Leah push the sofa against the back wall. Take the four of them, for instance. They couldn't have been more

3

different. Amy had dirty blonde hair which she was trying to grow out and green eyes like her grandmother's. She was pretty average in height and weight. Her worst feature, she thought, was her glasses which she had to wear because she was practically blind. She couldn't wait until she was old enough to get contacts.

Erin had dark brown eyes and short brown hair which she said she'd *never* grow out. She said short people looked better with short hair. Erin had been Amy's best friend since the fourth grade, when her family had moved to St. Louis from California. Erin was an amazing athlete for a tiny person. Robin said it was because Erin had lived in California for so long and everyone out there is into sports. Erin's parents had both been born in Mexico. At home, they spoke Spanish whenever they didn't want Erin or her brothers to know what they were talking about, but Erin said she could usually figure out what they were saying.

Leah was very tall and skinny with long, dark hair and blue eyes. People were always asking her if she was a model, which drove her crazy because she hated drawing attention to herself. You couldn't help it, though. Leah was a real artsy type, and so everything she did, from the way she dressed to

4

the way she thought, was different. She even went to a special private school, called the Day School, where she took art and music classes every day.

The fourth girl in the group, Robin, looked just like a Robin should look—bright red hair, freckles, and green eyes. She was also kind of plump and had a loud, chirpy voice. You couldn't miss her.

"What do you think, Amy?" said Leah, standing next to the sofa. "Is it too close to the window?"

"Further to the left," interrupted Robin, who'd managed miraculously to revive herself enough to find the diet sodas, cheezies, and licorice whips that Amy had stashed away for later.

Erin straightened up. "Boy, Amy," she said, "I can't believe how different it looks up here since Patrick moved out."

"It better," said Amy. "Patrick's such a slob it took me two days to clean it up."

Amy remembered when Patrick and her father had first decided to build the treehouse on the large branch of an oak tree in their backyard. It took them almost a whole summer, but Amy thought when they were finished that it looked almost as good as the treehouse in *Swiss Family Robinson*. To get inside, you had to climb up a six-foot ladder

5

which was nailed to the tree trunk. Then at the top there was a hatch in the floor which opened into the big main room. The room had walls, a ceiling, and even a cutout picture window. Over in one corner was another small ladder and another hatch door leading up to a small observation platform called the crow's nest. From here, you could see practically all of Washington Street, Amy's block. Across from the crow's nest, there was a spot where the tree trunk had been hit by lightning once and hollowed out. One person could squeeze in there pretty comfortably. Patrick had always called it the Cave, and he'd spent hours in there listening to his music tapes. Amy was thinking about renaming it the Conference Room.

"Are you sure Patrick isn't going to want this place back?" asked Erin, stuffing a fistful of cheezies into her mouth. "I can't believe he'd give it up."

"Positive," Amy answered. "All he cares about anymore is his motorbike."

"And Jenny Marconi," said Leah, who had perched herself on the sofa arm.

Everyone laughed as Amy settled herself into the desk chair, reserved for the editor, of course, and cleared her throat. "Okay. The meeting has now started. Our first edition is due this Thursday, so that Dad can take it to

6

his office Friday to make copies. We'll distribute them on Saturday." She looked up. "Any questions?"

Leah raised her hand. "How are we going to distribute them?"

"Easy," Amy answered. "We'll stick them on people's doorsteps." She paused. "How are you all doing on your assignments?" One thing Amy had done from the start was give everyone specific assignments. It made things run more smoothly and seem more like a real newspaper.

"I've already finished the map of the neighborhood and the banner design," said Leah, who was going to be the art director and news photographer. "Does anyone want to see the banner design?"

"Sure!" said Amy. The banner went on the very top of the newspaper and included the newspaper's name, the *Treehouse Times* and motto "All the News from Fillmore to Jackson Street." In Kirkridge, every street was named after a president.

Leah held out her sketchbook and the girls crowded around. "What do you think?"

Erin frowned. "Uh, are those hippos in high heels supposed to be our mascots or something?"

Leah shrugged. "If you want. I just

7

thought they were cute." Leah may have been the best artist in the neighborhood but you had to watch that her ideas didn't get too weird. One time she sprayed her hair green for St. Patrick's Day and it didn't wash out for a month. Another time she painted her bedroom ceiling black and added fluorescent constellations, which was fine, except the constellations were so bright they kept her up at night.

"Leaves or a treehouse would make more sense," Amy suggested, trying not to sound too bossy.

Leah looked insulted. "Leaves?" she said. "Plain old leaves?"

"Or a treehouse," said Erin. "How about that?"

Leah sighed and bent back over her sketchbook. In about thirty seconds she'd drawn a perfect picture of the treehouse. She'd even included the crow's nest.

"Perfect!" said Amy. Being the editor meant that she was in charge of the final decisions, which wasn't always easy. She turned to Erin, whom she'd asked to be business manager. "Any business to report?"

Erin shook her head. "Nothing so far. I think we have two advertisers. The Sugar Bowl and the copy shop." One of the things the girls had learned on their tour of the

Post-Dispatch was that newspapers get most of their income from advertising.

"I've chosen Janice Sloan to be Neighbor of the Month," said Erin. Erin and Robin were also going to be the feature columnists, which meant they both had special articles which they'd write for every issue. For now, the paper would come out once a month . . . unless something really exciting happened.

Robin slurped her soda noisily. "I've got a *great* scoop for my gossip column." She lowered her voice. "It's about Roddy Casper, the biggest greaseball of all time."

Leah wrinkled her nose. "Ugh. He is so disgusting. Remember that time he was fooling around with a Bunsen burner and he accidentally set his porch on fire? His grandmother looked like she was about to have a heart attack."

Roddy Casper lived next door to Amy with his grandmother and was also in the sixth grade at Kirkridge Middle School. He'd once told Amy that his parents were dead, but later Amy found out they were divorced. His mother lived in Chicago, where she worked long hours as a waitress. Amy felt sorry for him.

Robin leaned forward. "Last week Roddy got caught *shoplifting* at Korn's Drugstore."

"You're kidding!" said Amy. "What was he stealing?"

"Maybe a fire extinguisher?" Leah murmured.

Robin giggled. "My cousin Matt was there. He said Mr. Korn had Roddy by the ear and was squeezing him really hard. Roddy was yelling at him to stop. His ear had already started to turn purple when his grandmother—"

From below the treehouse, a loud cry suddenly filled the air. "You guuuuys. Come quick. Something's happened."

Leah swung her head out the window. "It's Chelsea Dale," she told the others. "World's biggest pest." In a loud voice she called back, "What do you want, Chelsea? We're very busy right now."

"But there's a police car in front of the drugstore," Chelsea said.

"Police car?"

Amy rushed to the window and pushed Leah aside. "Police car?"

Erin and Robin were already halfway down the ladder. "We'll go," Erin said. "Robin and I are the investigative team, right? That's what you said."

"All of us can help," said Amy, grabbing her notebook and wishing she hadn't told Erin that. "Come on, Leah."

10

Leah hung back.

"Come *on*, Leah," said Amy. "Don't be such a chicken. This may be our first real story!"

It wasn't far from Amy's house to the shopping area. Kirkridge, a suburb of St. Louis, had been built in the thirties and forties, but Amy's family had moved there only about six years ago. Her parents had said they wanted to be closer to the city, and Amy remembered how excited she was when she first saw the big old house with the rambling front porch and tree-filled yard.

Erin quickly sprinted ahead. "Wait for me," Robin called. "I'm your partner, remember?" She stopped to pop a caramel chewie into her mouth which didn't help her speed.

On the corner of Adams and Lincoln, a police car, its lights still flashing, was parked outside Korn's Drugstore. Erin ran back over to the girls. "I've already checked it out," she said breathlessly. "Follow me."

Robin threw out her arm. "Chelsea, you stay here. This is newspaper business. No fifth graders allowed." Chelsea made a face but stayed where she was.

Inside, two officers and Mr. Korn were talking to Roddy Casper over in the magazine corner. A small crowd had gathered on

11

the other side. Amy could see Roddy waving his arms and shaking his head back and forth.

"I knew it!" said Robin. "Roddy got caught shoplifting again."

"Shh," said Amy. "We don't know that yet." She turned to a boy she knew from school named Danny Clark. "What happened?"

"Mr. Korn thought he saw Roddy steal a pen," Danny told her, "but when he searched his pockets they were empty. So he called the police."

"What did the police do?" said Amy.

Danny shrugged. "Same thing. Searched him." He stared at Roddy. "Personally, I think he's innocent."

"Innocent!" said Robin loudly. "Roddy Casper? Innocent?" Several people looked at her.

"Robin!" Erin said. "We're supposed to be investigating, remember?" She turned politely to Danny. "Why do you think Roddy is innocent?"

"Because the police asked Mr. Korn if he wanted to press charges and he said no," Danny answered.

Erin looked at Amy who jotted a few notes on her notepad and nodded. Mr. Korn was famous for following kids around the store

12

whenever they came in. If someone even touched a magazine, Mr. Korn would yell out, "Are you planning to buy that?"

Amy leaned over to Leah. "Did you bring your camera?"

Leah nodded. "It's in my backpack," she said, taking it out.

"Take a picture," whispered Amy.

Leah stared at her. "Now?"

"You're the photographer," said Robin.

Leah hesitated. "What if he gets mad? I hate violence."

"He won't do anything," said Erin. "And if he does, we'll protect you."

Leah gulped and aimed. The flash hadn't even finished popping when Mr. Korn flew over and grabbed her by the arm.

"What do you think you're doing?" he said.

Leah turned white. "Ow! I'm from the news—"

Mr. Korn dragged Leah toward the door. "What do you think this is? A circus carnival?"

Leah looked helplessly at the others. "I was only trying to—"

"I know what you were trying to do," interrupted Mr. Korn. "Cause trouble." He waved his arm. "Just like all you kids.

13

Troublemakers, thieves. Everybody out." He shoved Leah through the door.

The girls rushed to Leah's rescue. "Mr. Korn," said Amy, "we're from the *Treehouse Times,* a new neighborhood newspaper, and we'd like . . ."

Mr. Korn's eyes narrowed. "Newspaper, huh? What kind of newspaper?"

"It's written by kids," said Amy proudly.

"Kids! I've had enough of kids!"

Amy felt her cheeks start to burn. "But we just want to find out what happened," she said.

"The store is closed," said Mr. Korn. He slapped an OUT TO LUNCH sign in the window.

Amy felt herself getting madder and madder. He had a lot of nerve insulting them like that. She felt Leah take her elbow and steer her toward the curb. "Come *on,* Amy," she whispered. "Do you want to be arrested, too?"

Outside, the crowd of people had already started to leave. "Creep!" Amy called over her shoulder. Leah looked like she was about to cry. "Sorry about what happened in there," she said. "Are you okay?"

"I guess," said Leah.

Minutes later, the two policemen came out, laughing and shaking their heads.

"*They* don't look too upset," Erin said.

"And they aren't taking Roddy with them," Robin added. She pointed at the door. "Look! Here he comes now. Let's try and talk to him."

"*I'll* do it," said Erin.

Robin pulled her back. "No, let me."

"We'll both go," said Erin.

"Here," said Amy, pressing her notepad into Erin's hand. "You might need this."

Roddy had yanked his leather jacket up around his ears that no one would notice him. "Hey, Roddy!" bellowed Robin.

Roddy ducked his head and began to walk quickly in the other direction.

"We want to ask you some questions," said Erin, starting after him.

"I'm late for karate," Roddy said. "Leave me alone."

Amy watched Erin and Robin disappear around the corner after Roddy. Beside her, Leah sighed and swung her backpack over her shoulder.

"I'd better go," Leah said. "I told Celeste I'd make dinner." Leah was the only person Amy knew who called her parents by their first names.

"What're you making?" Amy asked.

"Shrimp flautas," said Leah, "with green sauce."

"Sounds . . . interesting," said Amy. "So

15

long." For a few minutes, she stood by herself on the corner and waited to see if Robin and Erin were coming back. When it became obvious to her that they weren't, she started for home. She would try calling Robin later to find out how things went.

Amy had only gone about a block when she head a familiar cry. "Am-y-y. Come quick!"

Amy turned around to see Chelsea racing wildly toward her. "Now what?"

"You have to come back to the drugstore." Chelsea panted. Whenever Chelsea got excited her upper lip perspired.

"What's happened?" said Amy, breaking into a run. "More police?"

Chelsea shook her head and pointed. "Look!"

Amy stopped in front of Korn's drugstore and gasped. In the middle of Mr. Korn's window sat a brand-new sign. CHILDREN UNDER TWELVE NOT ALLOWED UNLESS ACCOMPANIED BY AN ADULT.

Amy wouldn't be twelve until next August. "He can't do that!" she said.

Just then, Mr. Korn stuck his head out the door. "Shoo," he told them. "Can't you read?"

"But Mr. Korn," Amy said, "a lot of kids use this drugstore."

Mr. Korn shook his head and pointed to the sign. "Not anymore they don't." And before Amy had a chance to say anything else, he slammed the door in her face.

Chapter Two

Amy marched along Lincoln Avenue, her mind in a fuzz.

"Now what?" said Chelsea, puffing up behind her. "Are you mad? Are you going to write about this in your newspaper?"

"Chelsea," said Amy with an exasperated sigh, "can't you see I'm thinking?"

Chelsea blew out her cheeks. "Look!" she said, pointing. "Robin and Erin!" She ran ahead, probably to blab the news.

By the time Amy caught up, Robin was already hysterical. "What do you mean, no drugstore!" she said. "That's where I buy my caramel chewies every day. How will I live without my caramel chewies?"

Erin rolled her eyes at Amy. "Maybe you

could try going without them," she said politely.

"Never!" said Robin, clutching her stomach.

"Well, maybe Mr. Korn will change his mind when he calms down," said Erin, changing the subject.

"No way," said Robin. "He hates kids. He's never smiled at me once."

"And he yells at you if you cut across his yard," said Chelsea.

"And he's never home on Halloween," said Robin. She suddenly gasped. "Oh, my gosh, I just thought of something else. This means I have to go all the way to the Stop and Shop across town when I want to buy my *Soap Opera Digest.*"

Amy started to get a little mad. "You're not the only person who uses the drugstore, Robin," she told her. "I happen to think I'm a very good customer."

"Me, too," said Chelsea. "I buy all my school supplies there, even though it's more expensive. They're the only place that sells those Unicorn and Rainbow Glo notebooks."

"True," said Erin. "And what about those cute teddy bear stickers? Everybody buys those."

Amy nodded and looked in the direction of the drugstore. "It's not fair," she said slowly.

"We have as much right to use the drugstore as grown-ups. Just because we're kids doesn't mean we automatically go around breaking things." She stared solemnly at the others. "I think," she said, "that the *Treehouse Times* has just found its first cause."

Two days later, Amy was working in the treehouse when Erin poked her head inside. "What are you typing, Amy?" Erin asked.

Amy looked up. "My editorial," she said. "Tell me what you think. 'Last Tuesday, a terrible thing happened to all the kids who shop at Korn's Drugstore. Because one kid was accused of stealing, we were all told we are no longer allowed in there without an adult. This newspaper thinks that is unfair. Most kids are polite and well-behaved. Besides, kids have rights, too!' Signed, Amy Evans, Editor.' "

Erin nodded as she dug through the soda cooler they kept in the corner. "Sounds great, Amy," she said, pulling out a cherry cream. "Short and to the point. Mr. Parkinson would love it." Mr. Parkinson was their English teacher at Kirkridge Middle School.

Erin threw some typed pages onto the table and then flopped herself down on the couch. "Are we lucky! Our first edition and we already have a cause."

"The whole neighborhood is talking about it," said Amy. "I can't wait until our paper comes out." She took off her glasses and cleaned them with a tissue. "I think we'll put Leah's photo and the story about what happened at the store right on the front page, where everyone can see it. My editorial will go on the back." She thumbed through Erin's work and found her Neighbor of the Month interview and the two ads she'd promised. Erin was so dependable. "Where's the story about Korn's?" Amy asked.

"Robin's bringing it. I interviewed everyone who was in the store and gave Robin that part of the story. Robin said she'd interview Roddy and finish the article with that."

Amy tapped her index finger against her glasses, the way she always did when she was concentrating. "Hmmm," she said, reading. "This Neighbor of the Month story about Janice Sloan is good." Janice ran a small daycare business in her house. The girls sometimes helped her out. "Did she really grow up in the house next door to her?"

"Yep," said Erin. "And the house she lives in now used to belong to her uncle." A little smile crossed her face. "Know what she told me? Mr. Korn was a pain when *she* was a kid, too."

Amy stared off into space, deep in thought.

22

"I wonder what Mr. Korn is going to do when he reads our paper?"

Erin shrugged. "Probably nothing. He wouldn't take a kids' newspaper seriously."

"True," said Amy. "But I keep hoping that after he sees our newspaper he'll change his mind and reopen the drugstore to kids."

"Don't count on it," said Erin. "A grouch is a grouch." She got down on her hands and knees and peered through the hatch. "I noticed one of the steps was loose. Want me to fix it?"

Without waiting for an answer, she swung herself upside down through the hole. "Somebody could get hurt on this," she called up. Erin was fast and wiry, and she could fix just about anything. "Where's everyone else?"

"Leah's in the crow's nest, drawing," said Amy. She paper clipped Erin's stories together and added them to the Done box. "As soon as Robin gets here Leah can do the dummy." The dummy was newspaper slang for the rough layout of the material on the page.

Erin's head popped back inside. "All finished."

From below, Amy heard Robin calling. "Hello up there. I'm coming through." Seconds later Robin's red hair appeared in the doorway. She heaved herself up and headed straight for the cooler. "What a day," she puffed. She unbuttoned the button on her jeans and collapsed onto the couch. "First, I got another D on a geography pop quiz, which means I'm grounded all weekend. No TV, no phone calls, nothing. Then, during cheerleading tryouts this afternoon my shorts split open. Lucky for me Mom hadn't done laundry in a while so I had on a bathing suit bottom instead of underwear." She sighed loudly and tore open a peanut butter cup. "If I don't make cheerleading I'll die."

"Why?" said Erin. "If you ask me, cheerleading is a waste of time. I'd rather play on the team."

"But it's a family tradition," Robin explained. "Felicia and Hilary would never forgive me." Robin's two older sisters were on the high school cheerleading squad.

"So?" said Erin. "You don't have to do everything they do."

Robin sighed. "You don't understand, Erin."

Amy interrupted. "What about the paper if you're grounded?" she said. "We were supposed to distribute it this weekend, remember?"

Robin threw up her arms. "Tell me about it. I tried begging, but Mom won't give in.

24

Grades come first. Before newspapers. Before cheerleading."

Amy nodded her head in sympathy. Grades had never been Robin's strong point. "Do you have your stories?"

Robin handed her two wrinkled paper towels. "Sorry about the stationery. We ran out of notebook paper."

Amy read the headline. "New Record Store Breaks All Records". She gave Robin a funny look. "Record store?"

Robin stuffed another peanut butter cup into her mouth. "Oh, I forgot to tell you," she said between bites. "Dad was invited to their grand opening yesterday. I guess it was because his shoe store is across the street. Anyway, I thought it was a good idea for a story so I talked him into taking me. You don't mind, do you?"

"I guess not," said Amy.

"I knew you wouldn't," said Robin. "Hey! You'll never believe who was there. The lady from the *Post-Dispatch* who gave us our tour. She was writing a story, too. She lives in Kirkridge. And look at this free poster I got. It's Melody Rollins."

Amy smiled politely. "I know."

Erin, who had been reading the gossip column on Robin's other paper towel, interrupted. "Excuse me, but I don't see our story

25

about Korn's. Leah needs it to do the dummy."

"Oh, that," said Robin. "Sorry. I decided not to finish it. I got too busy with this cheerleading thing. You guys don't mind, do you?"

Erin's whole body stiffened. "You mean you didn't write your part?"

"It was too hard," said Robin. "I tried talking to Roddy but he shut the door in my face. We can use the other story instead."

"But what about our cause?" Amy asked. "The drugstore? Remember?"

Robin gave them both an uncomprehending look. "We still have the editorial, right?"

"But it took me hours to interview all those people," Erin explained. She looked pretty upset.

"That's right," said Amy, jumping to Erin's defense. "You can't just decide not to write something without talking to us first. Our whole first page is planned around the other story."

"What's going on?" said Leah, climbing down from the crow's nest. She spied Robin's poster. "Oooh, Melody Rollins. I love her. Are we ready to do the dummy?"

"Not exactly," said Amy uncomfortably. She stared at Robin. "We're missing our lead story."

26

Robin stared back. "Don't use it, then."

"Wait a minute," said Leah. "Does that mean we can't use my picture? The one I risked my life for?"

"I still don't see what's wrong with the other story," Robin said. "I happened to work very hard on it."

Erin glared at her. "And *I* worked hard on the first story," she said. "The one we were *supposed* to write."

Robin looked helplessly at Amy. "I don't have time to write another story now. I'm already behind on my homework and I still have to work on my cheers."

Erin threw up her hands. *"I'll* write it then," she said. "Just give me back my part."

Robin squirmed uncomfortably. "I can't."

"Why not?" said Erin. By now, everyone was staring at Robin. No one wanted to see her ruin a good newspaper before it even started.

"Because," said Robin.

"BECAUSE WHY?" shouted Erin.

Robin's face got as red as a tomato. "Because I don't have it anymore," she shouted back. "Iggy chewed it up."

Silence.

"Iggy?" said Erin finally. "My story was

27

eaten by a hamster?" Erin looked like she was in shock.

"I let him out for a little exercise while I was doing my homework," Robin admitted. She paused. "Since Roddy wouldn't cooperate anyway, I didn't see any point in redoing the whole story. Can't we just use the other one?"

Amy shook her head. "It's not fair to the rest of us."

"Maybe Erin can remember what she wrote," said Leah helpfully.

Erin sighed. "Maybe."

Amy turned to Robin. "I'm sorry, but you have to finish that story. We had an agreement."

Robin slowly picked up her book bag. "Okay," she said evenly. "If that's what you want, you're the editor. I hope you realize, though, it's probably going to take me all night to get everything done."

That evening Amy was in her room working on her math homework when the phone finally rang.

"I'm finished," said Robin.

Amy felt a flood of relief sweep over her. She hadn't heard a thing from Robin and Erin since they disappeared right after the meeting. "Can you bring it over now?"

28

"I guess," said Robin. "But I can't stay. I haven't started my homework yet and my parents are breathing down my neck."

Amy hoped that Robin wasn't still mad at them. After all, it wasn't *their* fault Iggy ate the story and Roddy wouldn't cooperate.

Fifteen minutes later, Robin walked through the door and tossed her story on Amy's desk. "I hope this meets your approval, madam. For your information, it took me over an hour to find Roddy. He was mowing the Sondras' lawn."

"Did he talk?" said Amy.

"Not at first," said Robin. "I followed him back and forth until he did."

"Good work," said Amy. "What about Erin's part?"

"We figured it out," said Robin. "That took another hour."

While Robin sat and devoured breath mints, Amy read her story aloud. "On Tuesday, Kirkridge residents had some rare excitement." Amy looked up. "That sounds great!"

"It was Felicia's idea," Robin admitted.

Amy continued reading. "Mr. Korn of Korn's Drugstore thought he had a criminal in his store. Roddy Casper of 1466 Washington was accused of shoplifting a ballpoint pen. 'I didn't do it,' Roddy said, 'so the old toad had to let me go—' "

Amy gasped. "Robin! We can't print that!"

"That's what he said," Robin countered.

"But that's so mean . . . even if he *is* an old toad," said Amy. She ran her pencil through the offending word. "We'll change it to Mr. Korn." She pointed to a sentence a few lines down. "Do we know for sure Roddy was trying to shoplift the first time or was it also a false alarm?"

"Matt said he was shoplifting," Robin answered in an edgy voice. "Is that good enough?"

Amy shook her head. "Not really. Remember what we learned in school? You need at least two sources." She decided to change the subject. "What was Roddy trying to take the first time he was caught?"

Robin sighed loudly. "How should I know?"

"You could call Matt," Amy persisted, "or try talking to someone else who was there."

Robin gave Amy a discouraging look. "I suppose you want me to rewrite the whole story."

"No," said Amy. "It's good. It really is. I just thought these things would make it better, that's all."

Robin shifted around in her chair. "Listen,

30

Amy," she said. "I finished the story like you wanted, but now I really have to go. I still have lots to do and this newspaper isn't my whole life." She quickly left.

Amy sat quietly for a minute, drumming her pencil against her glasses. She picked up the phone and dialed. "Hello, Matt?" she said. "This is Amy Evans. I'm writing a newspaper article about what happened at Korn's Drugstore the other day. Do you mind if I ask you a few questions?"

The next day when Amy woke up it was pouring. Downstairs in the kitchen her mother was zapping some sausages in the microwave. "Lousy day, huh?" she said.

Amy stared bleakly out the window. "I hope it clears up by tomorrow so we can distribute our paper."

Mrs. Evans squeezed the grease out of the sausages with a paper towel. "Don't worry, it's supposed to." Amy's mother was an office manager of a realtor's office and worked most weekends, so she liked to pay attention to the weather report.

Amy looked out the window again. "Any chance you or dad could drive me to the bus stop?" On rainy days, Chelsea's mother usually let everyone at the stop wait in her van until the bus got there.

"Dad can drop you off," her mother said. "I'm not going in until later."

Not long after, Amy was sitting comfortably in the Dales' van, listening to a Melody Rollins tape in the backseat. Fortunately she had Erin to sit next to, because next to *her* was Chelsea, butchering every song. The van was pretty crowded and steamy, even though some of the boys like Grant Taylor and Roddy insisted on waiting outside.

"Did you get Robin's story?" Erin shouted over Chelsea's bad singing.

"Yes," said Amy. "But I still had to call Matt to get more information."

"What's with Robin anyway?" said Erin.

"I think she's nervous about not making cheerleading," said Amy. "Her mind isn't all here."

"You can say that again," Erin grumbled.

Erin's little brother Jamie turned around in his seat. "Who's mind isn't all here?"

"None of your beeswax," said Erin.

Jamie's nickname was Newsflash. You had to be careful what you said around him.

"Where *is* Robin anyway?" said Amy, looking at her watch. "The bus should be here any minute."

"Too late now," said Erin.

Everyone made a run for it as John, the bus driver, threw open the doors. "All

32

aboard," he shouted. The rain was coming down in buckets.

"Maybe Robin's sick," said Erin.

Amy looked anxiously over her shoulder. "Maybe," she said. "But she looked fine last night." They walked to the back of the bus where the older kids always sat.

John yanked the doors shut. "Let's go, kids," he yelled. John was the most popular bus driver at school. He'd graduated from Kirkridge High a few years ago and drove the schoolbus as a part-time job while attending the local college.

Amy and Erin settled into their seats and the bus took off with a roar.

Robin still hadn't shown up by the time the first period bell rang. "Good morning, folks," said Amy's homeroom teacher, Mr. Eric. Until last year he'd had a ponytail. Thank goodness he'd gotten rid of it.

Mr. Eric stuck his sneakers on his desk and called roll. "Evans, Feinberg, Flynn, Herman . . ." When he came to Robin's name and there was no answer, he stopped. "Anybody seen Robin today?" When no one responded he pulled on his beard and continued. "Wick, Warren, Young . . ."

A loud noise at the door disrupted the classroom. "Come on in," shouted Mr. Eric.

The whole class stared as Robin barged through the door. She was spattered from head to toe with mud. Water dripped off her nose. Her wet clothes stuck to her plump body.

Mr. Eric raised his eyebrows. "What's this? The creature from the black lagoon?"

The class burst out laughing. Robin's face turned bright red. "I missed the bus," she said. "I had to walk."

Mr. Eric shook his head. "Those are the breaks." He handed her a tardy slip.

"No fair!" said Robin. "I got there just as the bus was pulling out. I ran after it for two blocks but John pretended not to see me."

"That's not my problem," said Mr. Eric. "Please be seated."

Robin sloshed miserably across the room. Mud oozed out of her sneakers. She sat down with a loud squish next to Amy. "For your information," she whispered hoarsely, "if I hadn't stayed up until midnight finishing my homework, I would never have overslept."

Amy felt terrible. She really did. But what could she do?

"All right, class, let's settle down," said Mr. Eric. "We've all seen apparitions before."

Amy wasn't sure what an apparition was,

but she knew it wasn't too flattering. She scribbled out a note: "Sorry you missed the bus." Every time she tried to pass it, though, Mr. Eric seemed to be looking at her.

Finally, the bell rang. "Robin—" said Amy, getting up from her chair.

"Leave me alone," said Robin. "I'm not in the mood to talk." And before Amy could reach her, she hurried down the hall.

Chapter Three

"Well, what do you think?" said Amy. She was in the treehouse, leaning over the first official copy of the *Treehouse Times*.

"I think it's perfect," said Erin.

Leah squinted her eyes. "Me too. Except the picture of Roddy came out a little too blurry."

"That's the copy machine," said Amy. For the millionth time, she reread the headline: "Korn's Off-Limits to Kids." She slowly flipped through the rest of the three page issue—Leah's photo, Robin's gossip, Erin's Neighbor of the Month, Robin's record store story, her editorial . . . Not bad. Even her two-fingered typing job looked okay. She took a deep breath and picked up the bundle of papers. "Are we ready to pass them out?"

Erin nodded nervously. "This is *so* exciting, you guys. I can't wait to watch people read them, can you?"

"No," said Leah. Lately, Leah had started to wear all black. Black pants, black shirts, black sneakers. Everything. It drove her mother, who was a buyer for Saks, crazy, but Amy thought it made Leah look mysterious. "How's Robin doing?" Leah asked. "Anybody heard?"

"All I know is she went home early yesterday," said Erin. "I think she caught a cold walking to school in the rain."

"And nobody could call her last night to check up because she was grounded," Amy added. "Poor Robin. We have to remember to wave when we go past her house. I think she's still mad at us."

The girls climbed down the ladder and stood together in a little knot at the bottom. "Where to?" said Leah.

"May as well start at my house," said Amy. "Come on." The others followed as she ran through her backyard and up the steps to her front porch. "Ta da!"

As she started to place a paper on the doormat, Roddy Casper suddenly leapt out from behind a chair, scaring her to death. "Boo!" he cried.

"Eeek," screamed Amy. "What are you doing here?"

"Investigating," said Roddy. He grabbed the paper out of her hand. "What's this?" He saw his own face staring back at him. *"Aargh!"* He quickly read the headline.

Amy snatched the paper back. "Do you mind?"

"But that's *me,"* said Roddy, pointing.

"Obviously," said Leah.

Roddy glared at her. "I don't want my picture in your stupid paper."

"It's a free country," said Erin. "Besides, we don't say anything bad about you."

"Let me see that," said Roddy, pulling the paper back again. He started to read Erin and Robin's story, mouthing each word silently.

"Let's get *out* of here," Leah whispered into Amy's ear. "Roddy knows karate."

"No," said Amy firmly. "Let him finish."

Roddy finally looked up. "This is stupid," he said. "I didn't do anything wrong. The story says so right here."

"I know," Amy answered evenly, "but since you were the reason Mr. Korn closed his store to kids that still makes you part of the story." She clutched the rest of the papers to her chest. "Now if you don't mind, we've got work to do." She started down the steps.

"Wait," Roddy shouted after her. "I don't want to be in your paper. If you pass those out you'll be sorry."

Amy kept going. "No, we won't." To Leah she said, "Just ignore him. He doesn't know what he's talking about."

Leah looked back nervously. "Are you sure?"

"Positive," Amy replied.

With Leah and Erin helping, it didn't take long to finish the rest of Amy's block. Because it was still early, not too many people were awake yet.

At the end of the next street, Mrs. Sondra opened her front door to shake out a small rug. "Good morning!" all three girls chimed at once.

Mrs. Sondra gave a little jump and put her hand over her heart. "Oh," she said. "You startled me." The Sondras had lived in the neighborhood longer than anybody. Even their grandchildren were grown up. The thing most people remembered about them, though, was their garden. It had different color themes which went right through the summer. In the early spring it was all pink, then purple, then yellow, then pink again. Amy loved to walk past it to see which color was on display.

"Would you like a copy of our new neighborhood newspaper?" she said, running up the steps.

"What a good idea!" said Mrs. Sondra. "How much?"

Amy beamed. "It's free," she said. "Our costs are paid by advertisers."

Mrs. Sondra looked impressed. She glanced at the front page, at the picture of Roddy with the police. "Oh, dear, what's this?"

Erin jumped in. "Our cause," she said.

Mrs. Sondra looked confused.

"Korn's Drugstore doesn't allow kids under twelve to come in anymore unless they have an adult with them," Amy explained. "And it's all because of one incident."

"That doesn't seem fair," Mrs. Sondra said.

"It's not," said Amy. "That's why we're going to change things." Out of the corner of her eye she noticed a young man and woman walking past. Other customers?

On the sidewalk, Erin began gesturing excitedly.

Amy turned around. No wonder Erin was

excited. It was the woman from the *Post-Dispatch!*

" 'Bye, Mrs. Sondra," said Amy. She leapt down the stairs and ran after them. "Excuse me, please."

The woman turned around. She was small for a grown-up and had scraggly reddish brown hair and wire-rimmed glasses. "Yes?"

Erin was already at her side. "Remember us?" she said.

The woman looked at them both blankly. "Uh . . ."

"We're from Kirkridge Middle School. You gave us a tour," said Amy.

The woman smiled. "Oh, right. Now I remember."

Amy motioned to Leah to join them. "I'm Amy, and this is Erin and Leah." She pointed to Leah. "You don't remember her since she doesn't go to our school."

The woman nodded. "Nice to meet you again. I'm Vicky Lamb. This is Bill McKay, one of our photographers."

They were probably on their way to cover some exciting story, thought Amy.

"We heard you live around here," said Erin.

Vicky pointed to a little gray house up the block. "Right there," she said.

Amy's face lit up. "Then you must have

42

seen our newspaper," she said. "We just left one on your doorstep."

Vicky frowned. "Newspaper? I didn't see any newspaper."

"Maybe you stepped over it by accident," said Amy. She pulled another copy from her bag. "See? After we took your tour, we decided to start our own neighborhood paper. This is our first issue."

"The *Treehouse Times*," said Vicky, looking it over. "I love the name."

"Our office is in my treehouse," Amy explained. She pointed to the headline. "We even have a cause."

Vicky nodded. "So I see. How's it going?"

"We'll know after this issue," said Amy.

Vicky smiled. "Bill, we should get a picture of this. George will love it. A neighborhood newspaper run by kids."

"Who's George?" asked Erin.

"My editor," said Vicky.

Bill leaned over and took a big camera out of his bag. "Get in close, girls."

"We're going to be in the paper?" said Erin.

"Maybe," Vicky smiled. "Why doesn't one of you hold up the paper so we can all see it?"

Amy threw one arm around Erin and Leah

43

and held the paper out with the other. She made sure the headline showed, just in case.

Bill took two or three pictures. After that, the girls all gave their names and ages to Vicky. It was exciting to think they might be in the real paper.

As Vicky was leaving she said, "Let me know if you ever need anything."

"Gosh," said Amy, watching her go, "she's really nice." She turned to Leah and Erin. "Let's go check and make sure she got her copy on her doorstep."

They hurried back to Vicky's house. "It's not here," said Erin, who as usual arrived first.

"That's funny," said Amy. "I know I put one there."

Erin ran next door. "There isn't one here, either," she said.

"Or here," shouted Leah, from across the street.

Amy scratched her head. She was just about to ring a doorbell when she noticed Roddy, lying underneath a big maple tree across the street. Right away she knew what had happened.

She hurried over. "Uh, what do you think you're doing?"

Roddy lazily opened one eye. "What does it look like?" He closed his eye again.

Amy tapped her foot on the lawn. "You wouldn't happen to know where our newspapers disappeared to, would you?"

Roddy picked at his front tooth. "Nope."

Leah appeared. "Has he seen them?" she asked breathlessly.

Roddy laughed out loud.

"Oh," said Leah.

Now Erin showed up. She took one look at Roddy and said, "You're hiding our papers, aren't you, creep?" Roddy didn't answer. "You're going to get in trouble."

Roddy slowly sat up. "Yeah? What?"

Since none of them obviously knew what, Amy quickly said, "Let's go to the treehouse, guys." As they were leaving, she called over her shoulder, "You don't scare us, Roddy."

Back at the treehouse, the girls tried to figure out what to do. They were afraid they'd run out of copies. They had enough extra copies to replace the ones Roddy had snitched, but if he kept stealing them, they'd run out for sure. That's when Leah, usually the world's biggest chicken, came up with her brilliant plan. At least they hoped it was brilliant.

That evening after it had started to turn dark, the girls set out again. As they walked past Roddy's house, Amy said in a loud voice, "We'd better finish distributing these papers, guys, before it gets too dark to see." She stared at Roddy's front porch, where she was sure she saw a shadow move.

"Yes," shouted Erin in the direction of Roddy's house. "We'll start on ROOSEVELT STREET."

"ROOSEVELT STREET?" Leah blared. The shadow moved again.

The girls hurried on. It wasn't long until Roosevelt Street was almost finished. At the end of the block Amy noticed Leah stopped uncertainly in front of Mr. Korn's house.

"Psst, Amy," she called. "Should I give Mr. Korn a paper? He probably isn't going to like what we wrote about him."

"Leah!" said Amy. "How many times do I have to tell you? We're a newspaper. The whole point of a newspaper is to report the news."

"Okay, okay," said Leah, putting a paper on his porch.

After all the papers were passed out Amy said, "Time for Plan B." She turned to Leah. "Ready?"

Leah nodded bravely. "I can't believe I said I'd do this."

Amy and Erin disappeared around the corner, leaving Leah by herself.

For what seemed like forever, they kept

46

distributing newspapers, as if nothing were going on. Finally, it was time.

Very carefully, she and Erin snuck back to Roosevelt Street and hid behind a bush. Was their plan going to work? She felt Erin squeeze her elbow. "Here he comes," she whispered.

Just then Roddy snuck past, a bundle of papers already under his arm. Erin and Amy didn't dare breathe. They watched Roddy run from house to house, stealing every paper, until he reached the last house on the block. "Now!" whispered Amy.

As Roddy reached for the last paper, Leah suddenly popped out from behind a bush. "Smile, Roddy," she said, taking his picture.

"Hey!" screamed Roddy, dropping all the papers.

Amy and Erin raced over. "Aha!" said Amy. "Caught you!"

Roddy glared at them. "So?"

Amy held out her hand. "Picture, please, Leah." Lucky Leah had an instant camera. They couldn't have asked for a better picture.

Amy waved the evidence under Roddy's nose. "See this? It's going to be the front page of our next issue if you don't stop stealing our papers."

"That's blackmail!" Roddy shouted.

47

"No, it's not," said Amy. "It's news." She quickly picked up the stack of stolen papers. "And don't bother us again," she said. She was sure he wouldn't. At least not for a while.

Chapter Four

Monday morning, Amy and Erin stood waiting on the curb for the bus.

"Hear anything?" Amy asked.

"About what?"

"About the paper. Did anyone tell you they
liked it?"

"My parents," said Erin.

"They don't count," said Amy. She
glanced over at Roddy and Grant, who were
smashing sticks against a Stop sign. Good
thing there hadn't been any more trouble.

Just then Robin appeared for the first time
since Friday. Her nose looked bright red. In
one arm she carried a large box of tissues.
"Hi, everyone," she said in a miserable
voice. "How did it go?"

"Great!" Erin answered. She snuck a peek at Roddy and lowered her voice. "Remind us to tell you something later."

"What?" said Robin, honking loudly.

Roddy looked over. "I know you're talking about me," he said.

"No, we aren't," said Erin.

"Yes, you are."

"You guuuys." Chelsea popped in from out of nowhere and waved a copy of the *Post-Dispatch* in Amy's face.

Amy gasped. "Oh, my gosh! It's us. We made the front page!"

Suddenly everyone crowded around. "Look at my hair," groaned Erin. "It's sticking out everywhere."

"No, it's not," said Amy. "You look good." She squinted and read the caption: "Kirkridge residents Amy Evans, Erin Valdez, and Leah Fox took advantage of Saturday's good weather to distribute copies of their new neighborhood newspaper, the *Treehouse Times*."

"We're famous!" said Erin.

Roddy hooted. "That's a joke!"

Robin studied the picture and then sneezed. "Thanks for mentioning my name, guys. I'm grounded for one weekend and you forget all about me."

Amy shot Erin a glance. "That's not true,"

50

she said quickly. "We thought about you lots."

"Lots and lots," added Erin, not too convincingly.

"Didn't you see us wave?" said Amy. "We stood by your mailbox and waved when we were distributing the papers."

Robin sneezed. "No."

Amy changed the subject. "How are the cheerleading tryouts going?" Because the sixth graders were new to Kirkridge Middle School, the sixth grade squad was always chosen at the beginning of the school year, instead of at the end. The tryouts were led by the seventh and eighth grade squads.

Robin shook her head unhappily. "First cuts are this afternoon. I tried practicing in my room this weekend but my bed got in the way. I'm never going to make it."

"You'll make it," said Amy. "Don't worry. Haven't Hilary and Felicia been helping you?"

"Every night," said Robin glumly. "They're so sure I'm going to make it that they've already asked me to be this year's junior mascot."

Chelsea's eyes opened wide. "You mean the sixth grader who gets to cheer with the high school cheerleaders at all their home games?"

"They've already ordered my uniform," said Robin. "I was voted in unanimously." Robin groaned. "I told them to wait until I made the squad."

"That is so *cool*," said Chelsea. "No wonder you want cheerleading so bad."

Robin shrugged.

"What cheers are you going to do?" asked Chelsea.

"The usual," said Robin.

"Will you show us 'Two Bits Four Bits'?" said Chelsea.

"I guess," said Robin. She threw her book bag down next to the curb and ran to the other side of the street. "Two bits, four bits, six bits, a dollar!! All for Kirkridge stand up and holler!" She shot up in the air and kicked her legs apart, landing with a noisy thud. "Well? What do you think?"

"Pretty good," said Erin.

"I think I should try the kick again," Robin said. She started over, only this time Chelsea and two kindergarten girls joined in. "Two bits, four bits . . ." The bus pulled around the corner. Suddenly Robin's eyes grew wide. "Watch out!" she yelled.

But it was too late. With a big thump, the bus rolled right over Robin's book bag.

"Morning, kids," said John, throwing open the door.

Robin hurried across the street. "You just squished my lunch!" she yelled.

John leaned over the dashboard. "Where?"

Robin reached behind the front tire of the bus and pulled out her bag. A large black tire mark ran across the front. Something that looked like grape jelly oozed out of the bottom. "Ruined," Robin moaned. She unzipped the book bag and took out a soggy-looking math book, drenched with apple juice. A few pulverized potato chips floated to the ground. Robin peeled two caramel chewies off her history book. "My last ones," she said sadly.

John shook his head. "Sorry. I didn't see your bag."

"Next time watch where you're going," said Robin. She stomped to the back of the bus. "He did that on purpose," she told Amy and Erin.

"Come on, Robin. It was in the gutter," said Amy.

"He could have stopped," said Robin. "He's always picking on me."

Just then the bus started forward with a lurch. *"Oomph!"* Robin went flying through the air. "Help!" she screeched. She landed with a *kerplop* right on Roddy Casper's lap.

"Ow. Yuck," Roddy shrieked. He shoved

Robin to the floor and began massaging his legs. "Does anybody have a wheelchair?" he shouted. "I think I've been crushed to death."

Robin got up and angrily marched to the front of the bus. She gave John the evil eye. "You'd better stop picking on me," she warned.

John laughed. "I'm not picking on you," he said. "Sit down before you make me have an accident." He swerved to avoid a parked car. "See?"

Robin threw herself into the nearest seat. "You'd better be more careful," she told him.

John laughed again. "Yes, ma'am."

Robin stared out the window. Obviously, today wasn't going to be her day, either.

The first thing Amy always did when she got home from school was check the mail. After that she made herself a snack, usually potato chips and mayonnaise, and read through whatever looked interesting. Today, though, when Amy arrived home, there was no mail at all. Since her parents were still at work, she went to find Patrick. He was in the garage, listening to his favorite group, Sadistic Sister, on his tape deck and working on his motorbike.

"Did you see the mail?" she asked.

Patrick looked up. "Uh, yeah. It's in the family room." He bent over his bike again.

Amy wandered back into the family room, where she found the mail thrown in a pile on the sofa. Right on top she noticed her favorite catalog, *Today's Shopper*. It always had great gadgets like giant paper clips or personalized name plates for your desk. Whenever Amy had nothing else to do, she liked to go through it and pretend she was ordering things for her office. She'd even fill out the forms.

Underneath the catalog were some boring looking bills, a package of coupons, and one of those pictures of missing children. Then a piece of mail caught her eye. It was a long white envelope addressed to Miss Amy Evans, Editor, The Treehouse Times. Amy read the return address and gasped. "Oh my gosh! It's from Mr. Korn!" She quickly ran to the phone. "Erin, come to the treehouse right now," she said. "I just got a letter from Mr. Korn."

"What does it say?"

"I didn't open it yet. I'm waiting for you guys." She called Robin and Leah next. "Meet me in five minutes," she said. "It's an emergency."

Soon, everyone was assembled in the treehouse. "This better be important," said Robin, who had just gotten home from tryouts and looked tired and cranky. "I'm missing my favorite soap."

Amy waved the envelope. "This is it!" she said. "Our apology." She ripped the envelope open and read the letter aloud. " 'Dear Miss Evans, I was shocked to see such a prejudiced and one-sided view expressed in your newspaper.' " Amy gulped and continued. " 'Korn's Drugstore has been in business for thirty-eight years. During that time, many children have shopped here. Your newspaper made it sound as if my decision to restrict children was based on one isolated incident. This is not true. Had you looked into the matter, I could have shown you an entire shelf in my back office filled with items broken by children. I could have also shown you magazines with their covers ripped off, sticky fingerprints on my display cases, and empty candy wrappers littering the floor. No, Mr. Casper wasn't stealing anything this time, but that doesn't mean I haven't had countless other incidents where children took things without paying for them. In recent years, the situation has gotten worse. Children come into my store in little packs and act noisy, disrespectful, and obnoxious. I don't intend to reopen the store to children. Why should I? Next time, make sure you investigate both sides of a story before you write it. Signed, Henry C. Korn.' "

Amy angrily sat up in her chair. "What's *that* supposed to mean?"

"Did you hear what he called us?" said Leah. *"Children! Since when are we children?"*

"He doesn't know what he's talking about," said Robin. "I go in there all the time and never once have I seen empty candy wrappers on the floor."

"Me neither!" said Erin. "And I never heard of anyone stealing anything, either. He's probably making the whole thing up just to make us look bad."

Amy stared at Mr. Korn's letter. "I guess some people really don't like kids."

"You can say that again," said Robin.

The room grew quiet.

"Now what?" said Erin.

"Revenge!" said Robin. "I think we should go over there in the middle of the night and throw eggs at his window."

"Robin!" said Amy.

"Just kidding," said Robin. She stared at Amy. "So what *are* we going to do?"

Amy frowned. "I'm not sure yet," she said. "Let me think about it. The meeting is adjourned."

* * *

Amy sat in her room, thumbing slowly through the *Today's Shopper* catalog. She'd already spent about $500 on office equipment when she heard a knock on her door. "Come in." Her mother entered. "What are you doing home so early?" she asked her mother.

"It's 6:30," said Mrs. Evans. "I've been calling you to supper for ten minutes now. Didn't you hear me?"

"I had a lot on my mind," said Amy.

"Is something the matter?" asked her mother.

Amy handed her mother Mr. Korn's letter. "Read this."

"He sounds pretty angry," said her mother when she'd finished.

"Tell me about it!" said Amy. "What a grouch!!"

"What are you going to do?"

Amy pushed a fist into her pillow. "It's not my fault he doesn't like our paper. Nobody forced him to read it."

"He took the time to write a letter, though," said her mother.

"A stupid letter," Amy said. She folded her arms and stared at the wall.

"Did anyone interview Mr. Korn?" asked Mrs. Evans.

58

"No," said Amy. "But we talked to every-one else who was in the store."

Amy's mother shrugged her shoulders. "I should think that you would have wanted to hear his side."

"Mom!" said Amy, exploding. "He's a complete grouch! He hates kids!"

"He still deserves to be heard," said Mrs. Evans quietly.

Amy stopped. "Well, it's too late now," she said grudgingly.

Mrs. Evans smiled. "Is it?" She patted Amy's leg. "Come on. Supper's getting cold."

"I've been thinking," said Amy to Erin the next day during lunch. She watched Erin slather her taco in ketchup. "Maybe we should try to interview Mr. Korn."

Erin wrinkled her nose and took a big bite of her taco. "Are you kidding me?"

Amy shook her head. "I know he's a total creep, but what he said was right. We didn't tell his side of the story, and he deserves to be heard."

Erin made a face.

"I'm going over there after school today to interview him," Amy said. "Want to come?"

* * *

59

Later that afternoon, Amy and Erin walked slowly up Lincoln Avenue. From half a block away they could still see the sign in the drugstore window. "Are you sure you want to do this?" asked Erin.

Amy nodded and gulped. "You wait here," she said, stopping in front of the store. She took a deep breath and pushed the door open.

Inside, the store was empty except for Mr. Korn, who sat behind the candy counter, filling out some forms. Amy cleared her throat.

Mr. Korn looked up. "How old are you?"

"Eleven," she squeaked. Before Mr. Korn could say anything, she hurried on. "I want to apologize to you. I'm Amy Evans from the *Treehouse Times*."

"Hmph," said Mr. Korn.

"I want to interview you for our next issue. To be fair."

Mr. Korn waved her away. "I said what I wanted in my letter." He bent back over his work.

Amy stood very still.

"Go on," he said. "You don't need to talk to me. The matter is closed. I have work to do."

Amy could feel her cheeks burning again. "But don't you want—"

"Good-bye, young lady," he barked.

Amy slunk out of the store.

"What happened?" said Erin anxiously. "You look kind of pale."

"He won't talk to me," she said. "After all that, he won't talk."

"Now what?" said Erin.

"I guess we print his letter in our next edition," said Amy. "To be fair."

Erin didn't seem pleased.

"Don't worry," said Amy. "An Evans never gives up. The drugstore *will* open again."

"How?"

"You'll see," she said mysteriously. "I'll talk more about it at our next meeting."

Chapter Five

Amy sat by herself in the treehouse, waiting for the others to arrive. She checked her list of things to talk about one more time and made sure she had enough potato chips and mayonnaise.

Leah was the first person to show up. "Hullo," she said. She placed a juice container on the card table. "It's guava."

"That should be interesting," said Amy.

Leah twisted her hair up and around so that it all sat on top of her head. She anchored it with a pencil. "Know what I want to do for the next issue? A photo collage of the neighborhood. I just wish that photos reproduced better."

"They'll look fine," Amy reassured her.

"Everybody really liked the banner, too."
She paused. "How's school?"

"Okay," said Leah. "Tiffany and I are doing the scenery for the next play."

"Wow," said Amy. Leah's school did original plays all the time. Amy went once when Leah played a monarch butterfly in something called *What's Bugging You?*

Erin showed up next. "Whew," she said, climbing through the hatch. "I'm thirsty. Soccer tryouts were this afternoon." She looked around the room. "What's to drink?"

Amy pointed to the guava juice.

Erin poured a cup and gulped it down. "Not bad. Tastes like Gatorade." She wiped her forehead with the back of her hand. "Robin's still at cheerleading finals."

"I hope she makes it," said Amy. "We were trying to decide what to write about in the next issue. Leah's going to do a photo collage."

"Maybe Sandy Appleby can be Neighbor of the Month," said Erin.

"Sounds good to me," Amy said. Sandy lived next door to the Valdezes and worked as a carpenter. Erin had had a crush on him ever since she'd moved to Kirkridge.

"I saw your dad this morning," Leah told Erin. "He ran past our house."

"He's getting ready to run another mara-

64

thon," said Erin. "I never see him anymore. He's either at school or out running."

Amy sat up. "Let's write about him!"

"Dad?"

"Sure!" said Amy. "That's an interesting thing, and it's neighborhood, too."

Erin shook her head. "I don't think I want to interview my own dad. Besides, what's so great about running a marathon?"

"It's exciting," said Amy. "You train for months, right? Robin can help me."

"Help you do what?" said Robin, sticking her head inside.

"Interview Mr. Valdez," said Amy. "He's running in a marathon."

Robin giggled.

"What's so funny?" said Erin.

"Your dad is cute," said Robin. "I see him running past our house every morning."

Erin wrinkled her nose.

"How did tryouts go?" asked Amy.

Robin's expression changed. "We won't know until Friday," she said. "If you don't mind, I'd rather not talk about it." She blew her nose and looked around the room. "Anything to drink?"

Leah pointed to the guava juice.

"No diet soda?"

"Not today," said Amy. "It's Leah's turn to bring drinks."

Robin flopped down on the sofa without taking anything. As she fanned herself with her hand she said, "Did you hear? Mr. Eric lost a bet with one of the other teachers. He has to shave off his beard."

"No!" said Amy.

"I bet no one recognizes him," Robin said. "I'm going to put it in my gossip column." She paused. "I think I'm going to write something about John, too."

"Like what?" said Erin.

"Like how he's a bad bus driver."

Erin looked at Amy. "Since when?" she asked. "You can't prove that."

Robin stared. "Are you kidding me? Did you see how he made me fall the other day?"

"That's your opinion," Amy cut in. "It's not fact."

Robin held up her crushed book bag. "What about this?"

"It shouldn't have been in the street," said Erin.

"But he should have been watching where he was going!" said Robin indignantly.

Leah interrupted. "Are we going to spend this whole meeting arguing?"

"No," said Amy. She changed the subject. "I've decided to print Mr. Korn's letter in our next edition."

"Why?" said Robin.

66

"Because he's entitled to his opinion," Erin said.

Robin stared at her. "But his opinion is wrong."

"*I* know that," said Erin.

Amy intervened a second time. "That's why we need to change his mind about us. I thought maybe we could have a demonstration outside the drugstore."

"You mean like they do about nuclear energy?" said Leah.

Robin waved her hands. "I don't want to be arrested. My parents would kill me."

"We won't break the law," said Amy. "We'll just march around outside the store with signs. We'll need a lot of kids, though. The more the better. It makes us look serious."

Leah didn't look too thrilled, probably because she was still worried about violence. "Then what happens?" she asked.

"Hopefully we get Mr. Korn to change his mind," Amy answered.

"But what if he doesn't?" said Robin.

"Oh, don't be such a pessimist, Robin," said Erin.

Robin gave Erin a dirty look. "What's a pess-ma-mist?"

"Someone who looks at the bad side of things instead of the good side," said Amy.

67

"Are you accusing me?" said Robin.

Amy groaned. "You asked me to tell you what it meant. Give me a break!"

Leah put her hands over her ears. "Stop fighting, you guys!"

Robin scooped out the last of the mayonnaise dip with her finger. "If you want my opinion, a demonstration sounds stupid. Mr. Korn already hates us. Why should he pay any more attention if we march around with signs?" She picked up her things. "Are we done? I need to go home and soak my sore muscles."

"I guess so," said Amy. "What about Mr. Valdez? You want me to call him tonight?"

"See if he can talk to us tomorrow after school," said Robin. "Later, guys."

They all watched her disappear down the ladder.

"What's her problem?" said Erin after Robin had left.

Amy shook her head. "I don't know. Maybe she's nervous about making cheerleading."

"If you ask me, she doesn't seem that excited about being on the squad," Leah observed.

"Then she shouldn't try out," said Erin bluntly. "Nobody's forcing her to."

Amy paused. "Maybe not. But since Hilary

68

and Felicia are cheerleaders, she might feel pressured."

"That's no reason to take it out on us," said Erin.

"Maybe somebody should talk to her about it," said Leah.

"Yeah," said Amy slowly. "I think you're right."

Amy was the last person to arrive at the bus stop the next morning. In fact, she almost didn't make it because she was having a big fight with Patrick about who had accidentally left the freezer door open all night and flooded the basement floor.

"Wait for me," she yelled, when she saw the bus pulling up. She raced down the block in record time, just clearing the doors before John closed them. Robin was standing one person ahead of her.

"Move on back," said John. As Robin walked past him he reached down under his seat. "Here." He tossed her something.

"What's this supposed to be?" said Robin, catching it.

"A book bag," said John. "What does it look like?"

Robin stared at the bag, which was a very nice one. "Where'd you get it?" she said suspiciously.

69

"Heritage Bank was giving them out," said John. "Keep it."

Robin nodded. "Thanks," she grumbled, moving to the back of the bus.

"See that?" said Amy. "He's sorry about running over your book bag."

Robin only shrugged. "Maybe," she said. "But he can't make it up to me so easily."

That afternoon, Robin and Amy went to see Mr. Valdez at Kirkridge High where he taught biology. The biology lab was at the very end of the building. Amy remembered going there once before with Erin. They'd seen all sorts of creepy things like tarantulas, dissected frogs, and some frozen raccoons that were wrapped in newspapers in the freezer.

Mr. Valdez was grading some papers in the corner. "Hi, girls. You're right on time. Pull up some chairs." Amy and Robin crossed the room and settled in.

Mr. Valdez folded his hands and waited attentively.

Robin started to giggle.

"What's so funny?" he asked.

"Nothing," said Robin, still giggling. Amy hoped Robin's crush on Mr. Valdez wasn't going to make her act silly through the whole interview.

Mr. Valdez smiled. "Do you have any questions?"

"I do," said Amy. Each of them had made up four questions in advance. She read from her notepad: "Tell us about the marathon you're going to run. When is it and where?"

"I had the same question," Robin whispered.

"Don't worry, I have extras," Amy whispered back.

Mr. Valdez explained about the race, how it was in St. Louis in two weeks, and how it was his third marathon.

It was Robin's turn to ask a question next. "Does running help you lose weight?"

"Definitely," said Mr. Valdez. He'd just started explaining why when his phone rang. He talked for a minute and then put his hand over the receiver. "I'll be a few minutes, kids. Feel free to get up and look around."

Amy and Robin smiled and slid off their chairs. "Let's go see those raccoons again," said Amy, heading for the freezer.

"No way," said Robin. "Dead animals make me throw up." She stopped instead to stare at a human skull. Suddenly, she got a funny little grin on her face. "Amy!" she whispered. "Am I right or wrong? This looks just like Ms. Willis!"

71

"Shhh," said Amy, trying not to laugh. "We'll disturb Mr. Valdez."

But Robin couldn't stop. The more she tried not to laugh, the more she did. Pretty soon, Amy started to laugh, too. Robin was right. The skull *did* look like Ms. Willis, with her long, bony face and buckteeth. Every time Amy looked at Robin or the skull she cracked up all over again.

"I can't help it," Robin said, holding her sides.

"Robin! Cut it out!" said Amy, still laughing. She tried not looking at Robin, to make her stop.

"Girls, please," interrupted Mr. Valdez.

Amy pinched Robin's arm. "I told you," she said, managing to wipe the smile off her face. Out of the corner of her eye she noticed an old stack of yearbooks, sitting on the windowsill. She grabbed a few off the pile. "Let's look at these for a while."

The yearbooks were very old. Some of them probably went back to when Amy's parents were in high school. Amy and Robin began flipping through the pages.

"Oh, my gosh," said Amy. "Look! It's Miss Eareckson."

"With brown hair," said Robin. Miss Eareckson had taught English at the high school forever. Everyone knew her because she had a little dachshund named Hamlet whom she walked all over the neighborhood.

"Having fun?" said Mr. Valdez, standing over them.

"Where did you get these?" asked Amy.

"I'm the new yearbook advisor," he explained. "I was just going through them myself. Aren't some of the pictures comical?" He opened another yearbook and began to leaf through it.

"Wait," said Robin, suddenly throwing her hand across the page. "That's John McCauley, our bus driver!"

All three of them stared at the picture of the grinning boy. "Look at that cast," said Mr. Valdez. "Poor guy must have broken his leg."

A strange look crossed Robin's face. "I wonder how he did that?"

Mr. Valdez shook his head. "Don't know. Before my time."

Amy brushed Robin aside. "He was probably playing football or something," she said.

"You think?" said Robin. She slowly leafed through the yearbook index until she came to his name. "John McCauley. Lab assistant, chess club." She gave Amy a significant look.

"Girls," interrupted Mr. Valdez, "I don't

mean to rush you but I've got to be on the track field in fifteen minutes. Cross country meet tomorrow."

"Sorry," said Amy, shutting the yearbook. They quickly finished asking their questions, but Amy could tell that Robin's mind was elsewhere.

"What are you trying to prove?" she asked as she and Robin walked home.

Robin pressed her fingers into Amy's arm. "I bet he was in a car accident," she said. "That's how his leg got broken."

Amy made a face. "Come off it! Just because someone is wearing a cast doesn't mean they were in a car accident."

But Robin pressed on. "I can see it all now," she said in a dramatic voice. "It was a terrible, terrible accident. John was driving, of course. He was lucky he lived, but he made it. His license was suspended. His friends deserted him." She paused. "He gave me that book bag as a bribe so I wouldn't be mad at him and find out the whole gory story."

"Get out of here!" said Amy. "You shouldn't go around making things up like that. You have no proof whatsoever."

"Not now, I don't," said Robin, arching her eyebrows. "But I will."

* * *

Amy forgot all about John and Robin for the next few days because there was so much to do to get the next issue of the paper ready. Besides that, at school they were working on a big history project about the Civil War. The whole class had been divided into two sides, the North and the South, for a debate on the issue of slavery. Amy was head of the Southerners, which was hard because she had to argue *for* something which she was really *against.*

That's why she really wasn't paying any attention when Robin came over to her during lunch, grinning excitedly.

"Read this!" she said, shoving a piece of paper in Amy's hand. "I looked it up in the library."

It was a photocopy of a newspaper article from about five years ago. "Local Teen Charged in Accident," it said. With a sinking feeling, Amy read on. "A sixteen-year-old youth and his girlfriend were seriously injured in an auto accident on McKinley Street last night. Police say John McCauley, 16, and Bridgette Sullivan, 15, were driving east on McKinley when their car hit a telephone pole at the intersection of Harrison and McKinley. McCauley was charged with reckless driving. . . ."

"I told you he was a bad driver," said

Robin. "And this proves it! He shouldn't be allowed to drive a bus. I think we should write a whole big front page story about this, just like we did about Mr. Korn."

Amy stared at the article. "This is terrible!" she said finally. "Where did you find it?"

"I told you. I looked it up. One of the librarians helped me."

Amy scanned the article again. "I just can't believe John would do anything awful. Does it say here why he crashed?"

"Reckless driving," said Robin.

"But what made him be reckless?" Amy persisted. "Was he speeding? Or did he swerve to avoid an animal or something? Things like that happen, you know."

Robin frowned. "Stop making excuses for him."

"Hey, Amy," interrupted Dana Donley. "Where are you? It's time for our debate practice."

"Now?" she said.

"We really need to practice," said Dana. "We're about to lose the war again."

Amy sighed and then turned to Robin. "I think you should find out a little more about the accident before you write the story."

"Why?" said Robin. "It's all here in black and white."

Dana shifted impatiently from one foot to the other. "Come *on*, Amy," she said. "The bell is about to ring."

"All I'm asking," said Amy, "is that before you write this up you do a little more research." She lowered her voice. "This could be very serious, Robin."

Dana folded her arms and tapped her foot on the floor.

"Okay, okay," said Amy. "I'm coming." She turned to Robin one last time. "Can we talk about this some more?"

"I guess," said Robin. "I'll see you at the treehouse later."

That afternoon, Amy and Erin were standing on one side of the treehouse while Leah stood on the other. "What do you think?" Leah was saying. She held her photo collage aloft.

"Ummmm," said Erin.

"Stand back a little further," instructed Leah. "And squint your eyes a little bit."

"I don't get it," said Amy finally. "What's it supposed to be?"

"A tree," said Leah. "For *Treehouse Times.* Get it? All of the photos in the collage are pasted together to look like a tree."

Amy stared hard. "Oh, *now* I see."

Leah beamed. "Good idea, huh?" She

77

gathered up her collage. "I'll be in the crow's nest. I want to do a few more things to this."

Amy started to stop her. "Leah . . ."

"What?" said Leah, turning around.

"Oh, never mind," said Amy. She watched Leah climb upstairs. "What can she do to wreck a tree collage?" she said aloud.

"Plenty," said Erin, laughing.

Amy grew serious. "Robin showed me something today. It was a newspaper article about a car accident that happened about five years ago."

"So?" said Erin.

"The driver of the car was John McCauley," said Amy.

Erin's eyes grew wide.

"She wants to write a story abut it but I told her—"

"Yoo hoo," said Robin, climbing inside. She put her hands on her hips. "Well. I made it. I'm a cheerleader."

Amy forced a smile. Maybe this would take Robin's mind off John. "That's great! I knew you'd make it."

"You must be excited," said Erin. "This is what you wanted, right?"

Robin grinned. "I was the last person to get on. Hilary and Felicia have already said they'll take me to Aegean Pizza tonight to celebrate."

78

"When's your first basketball game?" said Amy.

"Who cares?" said Robin. "The important thing is that I made it." She reached into her book bag. "Here, Amy. I wrote up that thing for my gossip column that we talked about at lunch."

Amy shot a look at Erin and then read it aloud: "A certain Kirkridge bus driver may be in the wrong business. When he was in high school, he was arrested for reckless driving after being in a bad accident."

Amy looked up. "Did you talk to John?"

"I didn't need to. I don't mention his name."

"But everyone will know who you're talking about," said Erin. "John could lose his job over this."

"People have a right to know," said Robin. "What if John gets the bus in a big wreck and kids are hurt? Then what?"

"I see your point, Robin," said Amy, "but right now we're not even sure what happened."

Robin stared at her. "How can you say that? You saw the newspaper article with your own eyes."

Erin looked at Robin with disgust. "You're just trying to get back at John, aren't you?"

79

"I am not!" said Robin. "And how come you always side with Amy, anyway?"

Amy held out her hands. "Stop it, you guys." She waited until Robin and Erin calmed down. "All I'm saying, Robin, is that you have to do some more research before you write the story. Remember the story about Mr. Korn?"

Erin pointed an accusing finger at Robin. "That's the one you decided not to write, remember?"

"I wrote it, didn't I?" said Robin.

"Quiet, you guys!" said Amy. "It was *my* fault we didn't interview Mr. Korn. It was sloppy work." She took a deep breath. "And so is this if we print it."

"I disagree," said Robin. "Do you know how long it took me to find that article? No matter what I do around here, it's never enough."

The three girls stared uneasily at one another.

"Robin," said Amy finally, "I'm sorry to have to do this, but as editor, I refuse to print what you wrote until you can back it up."

Robin's face turned bright red. "You can't do that!"

"Yes, I can," she said.

Robin shook her head in disgust. "If you do that, then I quit."

"If that's the way you feel—" said Amy.

"It is!" said Robin, angrily heading for the ladder.

"Wait!" said Amy. She paused. "You won't tell anyone about John yet, will you?"

"I will if I want to," said Robin. "I don't work here anymore, remember?"

Chapter Six

Amy sat dangling her legs in the very top of the treehouse, thinking about all that had happened. It had been three days since Robin had quit, but it felt like forever. The first day after it happened, Robin just ignored them, but now it was getting worse. Today during lunch Robin said, "I'm thinking about writing up my story anyway. I bet the school paper would like to have it."

This bothered Amy a lot. Even if Robin wasn't working with them anymore, she still shouldn't write something that could cause so much trouble without checking the story further. Besides, Amy was sure Robin didn't care as much about John's driving as she did about getting back at him. But still, were they wrong *not* to write about him? What if he *did* have an accident and people found out about his record? Should she, as editor, look into the accident herself?

From the top of the treehouse, Amy peered down at the people below. Up here, you could see almost the whole length of the block. It was a great place for spying.

"Anybody home?" called Leah from below.

"I'm in the crow's nest," Amy answered.

Leah clambered through the hatch and squeezed in next to her. "What's happening?" she asked, adjusting her beret.

"Nothing," said Amy. "Mostly thinking." She poked at the tree bark.

"I brought all the stuff to make posters," said Leah. "Day-Glo, glitter . . . they'll be great."

"Have you seen Robin?" Amy asked abruptly.

"Not since she quit," Leah answered. "Why?"

Amy sighed. "Chelsea wants to know if she can have her job. We need more people."

"Oh, yuck," said Leah. "Anybody but her. She follows me around and tries to copy everything I do."

84

"She offered to help make the posters," said Amy. "I told her it was okay."

"You guuuys. I'm here!" shouted Chelsea, right on cue from the floor below. She cheerfully waved a few Magic Markers at them.

Leah made a face. "Do we have to?"

"Come on," said Amy, pulling her downstairs. "It's only a few posters."

Inside the main room, Chelsea was already filling in a sign which said, "Kids Have Rights, too!"

"Hey! That's mine!" said Leah indignantly.

Chelsea's face turned red. "Sorry. You want it back?"

"No," said Leah, sighing loudly.

Chelsea carefully added a few pink and gray swirls for decoration to the corner, the same way Leah had done on the other ones.

Leah took another poster and sat with her back to Chelsea.

"I told everyone I know about the demonstration," Chelsea said, still drawing. "I bet we have a million kids show up."

"I hope so," said Amy. "A million kids would be nice."

Erin came crawling up the ladder. "Here's the flyers," she said. She made a funny face. "Something weird happened on my way here. I ran into Roddy and Grant and Roddy asked me if he could have a flyer.''

"Did you give him one?" said Amy.

Erin nodded. "He'd have gotten one anyway when we pass them out at school tomorrow.''

"I wonder what he wanted?" said Leah.

Amy shrugged. "I don't know. Maybe he wants to march with us.''

The next morning at school, everyone was bunched around the lobby when Amy got off the bus. "What's going on?" she said, moving toward the crowd.

"Grant and Roddy brought a snake," said Pia Bailey. "He's six feet long.''

Amy pushed through the people.

Over by the library, Roddy was trying to lift an enormous wire cage. "Move back, out of the way," he shouted.

The principal, Mr. Bottomly, walked in. "What's going on here, boys?" he said.

"We're taking Roddy's snake to the science room today," said Grant.

Mr. Bottomly peered into the cage.

"It's a boa constrictor," Roddy told him. "I got it for my birthday.''

Mr. Bottomly nodded. "Is he dangerous?''

"He eats live mice," said Grant.

Several kids gasped.

Mr. Bottomly frowned. "Did you boys get permission to bring this snake to school?"

"Mr. Eric said it was okay," said Roddy. "His name is Crusher." The crowd oohed a few more times.

"Let them have some room, boys and girls," said Mr. Bottomly as Roddy and Grant picked up the cage once again.

"Disgusting, don't you think?" whispered someone into Amy's ear.

"Robin!" said Amy. Robin had hardly said a word to her since she'd quit. She wondered what she wanted. Maybe she'd changed her mind about everything.

"I heard Chelsea asked for my job," she said.

"We didn't give it to her yet," said Amy.

"You can if you want to," said Robin.

"Oh," said Amy, trying not to look too disappointed. "How's cheerleading?"

"Okay, I guess," said Robin. "It's a lot of exercise, but at least Felicia and Hilary are off my back." She started to walk away and then turned around at the last minute. "Oh, I almost forgot to tell you. I'm going to talk to the school newspaper today after school."

"What about?" said Amy, as if she didn't already know.

"About John," Robin answered. "What else?"

87

Amy stared helplessly. "Are you sure?" she said finally. But it didn't matter. Robin had already disappeared.

Because the next day was Saturday, the day of the demonstration, Amy didn't have much time to worry about Robin. She and Leah and Erin spent the whole afternoon finishing posters and making plans. Erin had even managed to borrow a megaphone from her father, and after a few fights about who was going to get to use it, they decided to take turns.

At ten o'clock on the dot the next morning, Leah and Erin stood anxiously waiting at the foot of the treehouse. Erin's little brother Jamie was in charge of guarding the posters and the megaphone until they got started.

"Where is everyone?" said Erin. "I thought we said ten o'clock."

"Maybe people thought we were supposed to meet at the drugstore instead of the treehouse," Leah said.

Just then two little boys who were friends of Jamie's showed up. "We came to march," said one of them.

"Will we get arrested?" said the other one. "I want to ride in a police car."

"This isn't the kind of demonstration where people get arrested," said Amy.

The boys looked disappointed.

Amy bent down. "Do you know why we're marching?"

The boys shook their heads. "We came because Jamie told us to," said one.

"We're protesting because we think kids should have rights too," Amy said. "How would you like it if somebody told you that from now on, only girls could have recess?"

"I'd be mad," said the first boy. "That's not fair."

"And how would you feel if they said the *reason* was because all boys are bad students?"

"That's not true," said the second boy. "There's only a few bad students in our room."

"Well, this is no different," said Amy. "Someone is saying that just because we're kids we don't deserve to be treated the same as everyone else."

A few more kids showed up, including Chelsea, who had on a beret like Leah's. "We want in, we want in," she chanted, marching up to the tree.

"Get me out of here," muttered Leah.

By ten-fifteen there were about twenty kids waiting around. "Okay," said Amy to Erin. "Let's get ready." While Leah passed out the posters, Amy gave instructions through the

89

megaphone. "Everybody line up please," she shouted. "We're going to march two by two, so find a partner."

There was a lot of confusion but finally everyone was ready. Amy took her place at the head of the line.

Slowly, the demonstration moved toward the sidewalk and started to make its way up the block. The marchers had only gone a few yards when suddenly Roddy and Grant screeched out of nowhere on their bikes.

"Halt!" yelled Grant, blocking the marchers' path.

The marchers ground to a stop.

Amy's heart started pounding. What could Roddy want?

Roddy got off his bike and faced the crowd. "Ladies and gentlemen. Boys and girls. In a few minutes a spectacular event is going to happen. My boa constrictor, Crusher, is going to swallow his first large mouse . . . *alive.*"

The crowd buzzed with interest.

"Cool!" said Michelle.

"Can we watch?" asked a boy named Gary.

Roddy took one look at Amy and then nodded triumphantly. "Right this way!"

He turned the opposite direction from the drugstore. Amy watched in amazement as the whole crowd started to follow him down the block, just as if he were the Pied Piper. "Wait!" she cried.

Everyone stopped again. "The drugstore is important," she pleaded. "We need you."

"Why?" said Michelle.

"Because we want to show Mr. Korn how we *can* be responsible."

"But I'd rather watch Crusher swallow a mouse," said a third grader named Kate. "It sounds like more fun."

"Me too!" said a little boy wearing a baseball cap.

Roddy looked at his watch. "Better hurry," he said. "Crusher only gets one mouse a month. You don't want to miss it."

Amy angrily walked over to Roddy. "You did this on purpose!"

Roddy threw up his arms. "Who, me?"

Erin butted in. "Don't you care about being able to go to the drugstore?"

Roddy grinned. "I can go anytime I want," he said. "I'm twelve now."

Amy's eyes narrowed. So that was it. Now that Roddy knew he could get into the drugstore, he was going to do everything he could to ruin it for the rest of them.

Amy looked around. Most of the kids had already disappeared around the corner with Grant.

91

"Roddy Casper," she said. "That was a dirty trick!"

Roddy just laughed. "I told you not to print that story about me," he said, climbing onto his bike.

Amy watched him leave.

"Creep," yelled Erin after him. She stood protectively next to Amy. "Don't worry, Amy. We'll get him back."

Amy shook her head and sadly surveyed the damage. Besides themselves, there were only two little second grade girls left. "We're afraid of snakes," one of them said. "Can we still march?"

Amy sighed. "I don't think so. Not today." On the sidewalk, all the posters they'd worked so hard on lay in a sad little heap.

"Why don't you go?" said Amy to everyone. "No point in sticking around." She bent over to pick up the posters.

"Amy?"

Amy turned around and saw Vicky Lamb, the reporter from the *Post-Dispatch*. "Oh, hi," she said glumly.

"Hi there," said Vicky cheerfully. "How's your paper doing? I noticed the sign is still in the drugstore window."

Amy felt a knot start growing in her throat. "I know," she said.

Leah put her arm around Amy's waist.

92

"We were just on our way to the drugstore to demonstrate when this crudface named Roddy stole everybody away."

Amy wiped her cheek. Vicky probably thought she was a big baby. She was so disappointed, though. She felt like she was the only one who really cared about what happened at the drugstore.

Vicky nodded sympathetically. "I'm sorry to hear that."

Amy didn't want to have to say anything else because she was sure she would really start bawling. Instead, she picked up the last poster. "Gotta go," she said stiffly.

"Have you tried talking to Mr. Korn personally?" Vicky asked.

"She did that already," said Erin. "He doesn't want to talk to her."

"He wrote me a letter," Amy said. She explained the whole story.

"Would it help if I went with you?" said Vicky.

Amy shook her head. "I don't think so."

"But maybe if you had an adult along, he would be more inclined to take you seriously. It can't hurt."

Amy didn't feel convinced.

"I think you should go," said Erin.

"You do?"

"It'll make you feel better."

"But what will I tell him?"

"Tell him what you told me," said Vicky. "That just because you're kids you still have rights. And you can still be responsible."

Amy slowly nodded. "Okay," she said finally. "I'll go. I hope this works, though. I don't want to embarrass myself again."

Vicky took her arm. "Sometimes we need to be a little persistent to get something we care about. No need to be embarrassed about that."

They headed up the block, arm in arm.

Chapter Seven

All the way to the drugstore, Vicky told funny stories about her cats—Horace, Wendell, and Willkie—which helped put Amy in a better mood and took her mind off being nervous. When they got to the store, Vicky said, "Ready?"

Amy nodded her head and went inside. Today the store seemed to be much busier than last time. Amy counted about six customers, not including them. Over by the cash register, Mr. Korn was talking to a man holding a long clipboard. It must have been an important conversation since he hadn't even noticed the two new customers.

"Henry," the man was saying, "I know

you're usually good for twelve cases but we've got a new policy."

Mr. Korn looked annoyed. "What is it?"

The man wrote something down on his clipboard, unloaded some cartons which had caramel chewies written on the side, and handed the clipboard to Mr. Korn to sign. "Gotta buy fourteen cases to qualify for the discount now."

Mr. Korn sighed. "So give me fourteen," he said. He signed the clipboard and handed it back. "I hope I can sell all these."

"You will," said the man. "See you next month."

Amy was so busy listening that she forgot to be nervous. As soon as the man left, she walked over to Mr. Korn and said, "I bet if you allowed kids in here you'd sell more candy."

Mr. Korn peered over the counter. "You again! Where's your adult?"

"Right here," said Vicky, rushing to her side. She stuck out her hand. "Vicky Lamb. *St. Louis Post-Dispatch.*"

Mr. Korn's eyebrows went up.

Amy drew a deep breath. "Mr. Korn, I came back because I had something else to say. I'm sorry you've had so many problems with kids in your store, but I think you're being unfair. *Most* kids are responsible."

96

Mr. Korn leaned down. He was so close Amy could smell his breath, which smelled like sour postage stamps and tobacco. "Young lady," he growled, "it is fully within my constitutional rights as an American citizen to decide who can and can't come into my store."

Amy shot a desperate look at Vicky, who came to her rescue. "Mr. Korn," Vicky said, "no one is denying you your rights. We're just asking you to reconsider your position."

Mr. Korn stubbornly shook his head. "My position remains the same." He moved out from behind the counter. "Excuse me, but I have customers who need help."

Vicky put her hand on Amy's arm. "Let's go," she said quietly. "We'll talk more outside."

"What a grouch!" Amy exploded when they stepped outside.

"Not the most pleasant man I ever met," Vicky agreed. She smiled at Amy. "You gave it a good shot, though. You really tried."

"Is that it?" said Amy. "Isn't there something we can do?"

Vicky sighed. "I'm afraid he has this notion in his head that all kids are reckless and irresponsible."

"We'll change his mind, then," said Amy. "We have to be persistent, right?"

Vicky smiled. "I like your style. Any ideas?"

Amy thought for a moment. "Not yet." She gazed at the window. "I'm going to think of something, though. I'm not ready to give up yet."

After Amy left the drugstore, she wandered along Adams Street by herself for a while, not really heading in any particular direction. As she passed the pizza parlor she remembered she hadn't eaten any lunch yet. She reached into her kneesock, where she'd stuffed a few dollars this morning before the demonstration. Amy prided herself on always being prepared.

"Ahh, it's Miss Pulitzer," said Mr. Petropoulus, the owner, as she came through the door.

Amy smiled. Calling her "Miss Pulitzer" was a little joke she and Mr. Petropoulus had. The Pulitzer Prize was an award given for excellence in newspaper journalism. "May I have one slice with anchovies, please?"

Mr. Petropoulus wrinkled his nose. "Anchovies? A nice girl like you?"

Amy laughed and then sat down on a stool near the front to wait. While she waited, she studied all the postcards from Greece that Mr. Petropoulus had taped on the wall. He'd once told her they were pictures of the place he'd grown up.

Out of the corner of her eye, Amy saw a familiar face.

"Hi," said Robin, plopping down beside her. She was wearing her new cheerleading uniform.

"Hi," said Amy, not very enthusiastically. She wondered why Robin was being so friendly.

"How did your demonstration go?"

"It didn't," Amy answered. Before Robin could start asking questions she added, "And I'd rather not talk about it."

They sat in silence until finally Amy said, "How's cheerleading?"

"Great!" Robin answered. "I quit!"

Amy gasped. "You did? Why?"

Robin grinned. "I started thinking. I hate to exercise. I hate cold weather. I hate Lark Hogan, who by six votes to one got elected head cheerleader. And most of all, I hate the idea of being junior mascot. I'm not even sure how you *play* football." She pointed to herself. "Tell me the truth. Do I look like a junior anything?"

Amy shook her head politely. "Why did you make such a big deal out of making the squad, then, if it's not what you wanted?"

"Big sister pressure," said Robin. "They

expected me to make the squad to preserve the family name. It was making such a grouch out of me, though. I finally realized that I'd proved to them I could do it, and that's what counted."

"So what happened?" said Amy.

Robin smiled slyly. "This morning, when Lark yelled at me for the ten millionth time about kicking my legs higher, I finally got my revenge. I told her to drop dead."

"Robin!"

Robin burst out laughing. "I haven't felt this great for weeks! They were all jealous of me, anyway, because I was junior mascot. Now Lark can be junior mascot and spend every weekend freezing her tail off."

Mr. Petropoulus came over. "You want a slice, Red?"

"Yes, please." Robin scanned the candy display. "And a package of licorice. I worked up an appetite this morning."

Amy hesitated for a second and then said, "By the way, what did the school newspaper say about your story about John?"

Robin shrugged. "Oh, *that*. I've been so busy with cheerleading . . ."

"Are you going to write it or not?" Amy demanded.

Robin squirmed uncomfortably in her seat. "Well . . . I'm not sure—"

"Why not?" said Amy.

"Look!" said Robin. "Pizza's here. Dig in, Amy."

Amy couldn't help being curious. It wasn't like Robin, the biggest blabbermouth of all time, to be so vague. And why was she hanging around her like this? She stared at Robin as Robin bit into her pizza.

Robin slowly turned. "Do you mind? I'm trying to concentrate on my lunch."

"Sorry," said Amy, "but I sort of can't help it." She was just about to pursue Robin some more when she noticed the man with the clipboard who had just been talking to Mr. Korn come into the pizza parlor.

"Afternoon, George," the man said. He unloaded a handcart full of mint and candy boxes and then scribbled a few notes on his clipboard. He handed the clipboard to Mr. Petropoulus. "George," he said, "I know you usually take ten cases but we've got a new company policy. You have to buy twelve cases to get a discount now."

Amy stopped chewing.

Mr. Petropoulus threw up his hands. "How am I gonna sell twelve cases of candy in a pizza shop?"

The man shrugged. "You want the discount, don't you? Sign here."

Amy frowned. Something wasn't right.

101

Hadn't that man just told Mr. Korn he had to buy *fourteen* cases to get a discount? Why would it be any different for Mr. Petropoulus? As the man headed out the door, Amy pulled on Robin's arm.

"What is it?" said Robin.

"I have to check on something," Amy told her. "I'll be right back."

Robin slid off her stool. "Wait for me."

Amy didn't have time to think about Robin. She hurried out, with Robin following, and watched the man climb into a truck with H & M Distributors written on the door. The truck slowly drove down the block and stopped again in front of the Sugar Bowl.

"Oh, good," said Amy, heading down the block. "I was hoping he'd stop there."

"What's this all about?" said Robin, wiping her lips.

"I'm not sure yet," said Amy. She stood in front of the Sugar Bowl and pretended to study the menu in the window as the man unloaded more candy cartons and wheeled them into the store.

"Afternoon, Kay," he said. He checked his clipboard and then said, "Sorry to tell you this, but you're going to have to buy fifteen cases from now on to get the discount."

Amy nudged Robin's arm. "See! This time he said *fifteen* cases."

"I don't get it," Robin whispered.

Amy motioned her aside. "How come he's telling everyone something different?"

"I don't know."

"I don't either," said Amy. "But I'm going to find out." She headed toward her house.

"Wait," said Robin. "Can I come?"

Amy hesitated. "If you want."

As they walked, they talked about what had happened. "What I need to do," said Amy, "is try and figure out why everyone is getting a different discount."

"Why don't you call the candy company and ask them?" said Robin.

Amy looked at her. "That's a great idea! What should we say? We don't want them to suspect anything."

"I have an idea," said Robin. She ran into Amy's kitchen. "Where's your phone book?"

"In that first drawer next to the sink. Wait until I get my notebook, though."

"Right," said Robin.

Now they were organized. Robin stared at the phone book. "Uh-oh. Who do we call?"

"The name on the side of the truck was H and M Distributors," said Amy. "Let's try that." She leafed through the phone book. "Found it!" She handed the phone to Robin.

Robin cleared her throat and dialed. "I

hope they're open on Saturday," she said. "Hello? May I speak to someone about buying candy?" She paused. "Hello. I'm calling from Kirkridge Middle School. Our school store wants to sell candy this year. How do we get a discount?" She listened. "We have to buy at least ten cases?"

Amy whispered, "Ask him if that's the discount for everybody."

Robin nodded. "Does everybody get a discount after ten cases? Like pizza stores and stuff like that?" She moved her head up and down. "All discounts start after ten cases. Okay, thank you. We'll call back with our order later." She hung up. "Now what?"

Amy drummed her pencil on the table. "Why would someone lie about how many cases you needed for a discount?"

"Is there anyone we can ask?" said Robin.

Amy's face lit up. "I bet Vicky would know!"

Five minutes later, Robin and Amy were standing on Vicky's doorstep, explaining the whole story. "Good detective work!" she said when they finished. "Sounds like the salesman is trying to get the store owners to buy more candy so that he'll get a bigger commission."

Amy nodded. "Is he breaking the law?"

"Not really," said Vicky. "But he *is* misrepresenting the company, which is wrong."

"I don't get it," said Robin. "What's he doing that's wrong?"

Vicky explained. "The candy salesman gets a commission or percentage on everything he sells, which is how he makes his salary. Let's say, for example, that every time he sells a case of candy, the company gets nine dollars and he gets one dollar. Now, he knows that Mr. Korn usually buys ten cases of candy, right? But if he can convince Mr. Korn to buy twelve cases, that means that he makes an extra two dollars."

"And he convinces him by telling him he won't get a discount unless he buys more!" said Amy.

"Right," said Vicky. "The store owner wants the discount because the less he pays for the candy the more he makes when he sells it to you."

Robin scratched her head. "This is confusing."

Vicky laughed. "It is, isn't it?"

Amy said, "Do you think we could write a story about this?"

"You bet!" said Vicky. "Those store owners are going to be good and mad when they find out they were tricked into buying more candy."

"I have the perfect headline," said Robin. "Local Store Owners Sour on Sweets!"

"I love that," said Amy. "Let's go to the treehouse and write it up."

They waved good-bye to Vicky and rushed off. It wasn't until they were half-way up the block that Amy realized something. "Hey, I thought you'd quit," she said suddenly.

Robin blushed.

"That's okay," Amy said. "I was hoping you'd come back." She decided not to ask about John again. Not today, anyway.

Chapter Eight

As soon as Amy and Robin got back to Amy's house, Amy called the distribution company again to make sure they had their information straight.

"Do you think we should tell them what's going on?" Robin said while Amy was dialing.

"Why not?" Amy answered. "They'll probably be happy we discovered this."

But when Amy got the same man on the phone whom Robin had talked to and explained the whole story, instead of being overjoyed he said, "Are you sure you didn't make this up?"

"Of course I'm sure!" Amy answered indignantly. She hated it when adults treated her like she was brain dead.

The man paused. "Then how come you're so interested?"

"We're going to write this up for our neighborhood newspaper," said Amy.

"Newspaper!" the man yelped. "You're from a newspaper? Why didn't you say so? You can't print something like this in a newspaper, for God's sake."

"Why not?" said Amy.

"Because it'll make us look bad," he shouted. He stopped for a moment and then continued in a calmer voice. "Young lady—"

"It's Amy," she cut in. "Amy Evans."

"Amy. I tell you what. I'll get our guy to stop, okay? Then you won't need to write your story."

Amy put her hand over the mouthpiece to talk to Robin. "He doesn't want us to write the story," she whispered. "He promised to get the man to stop."

Robin frowned. "Is that okay?"

Amy uncovered the mouthpiece. "Can we call you back?"

"Absolutely, absolutely," said the man. "It's Vincent Capiello."

Amy hung up the phone and dialed again.

"*Now* who are you calling?" said Robin.

"Vicky," answered Amy. "She'll know what to do."

Just as Amy predicted, Vicky was on their side. "A newspaper shouldn't worry about whether it's hurting someone's image or not," she told Amy. "If you feel that what you've discovered is newsworthy, that your readers will be interested in knowing about it, then you should go ahead and print it. Just make sure you're accurate. Have you spoken to the store owners?"

"Not yet," said Amy. Just then a thought occurred to her. She was surprised she hadn't thought of it before. "Could this make Mr. Korn change his mind about kids?"

"It could, but . . ." said Vicky. Amy waited for Vicky to say something more, but she didn't. Maybe she wanted Amy to figure it out on her own.

"Okay, then," said Amy. "Thanks for the advice." She hung up the phone.

"Well?" said Robin. "Do we write it or not?"

"We write it," Amy said. She collected her notebook and pen. "Let's go talk to the store owners."

They went to see Mr. Petropoulus and Kay first, saving Mr. Korn for last. As soon as Amy told Mr. Petropoulus what was happening, Mr. Petropoulus picked up the phone and called the company. "What's this I hear about my discount being ten cases, not twelve?" he shouted into the phone. "Never mind who I heard it from. That weasel Walter had better start watching his step." He slammed down the phone.

At the Sugar Bowl, Kay was even angrier. "Every month he's shown up in here telling me the discount has gotten higher." She called the distribution company. "I'd like to cancel my contract, please," she said. "It's not important who told me. All I know is I have enough candy here to last the rest of the year."

Amy scribbled furiously. They were getting some great notes.

At last it was time to go see Mr. Korn. When they got to his store, the sign was still up. Amy looked at Robin and then marched bravely inside.

"I'll do the talking," she said to Robin. "He knows me."

Mr. Korn was standing right inside the door. Amy quickly pulled out her notebook. "Mr. Korn—"

"No comment," he interrupted.

"But this is about something else," Robin cut in. "We think you're being cheated."

Mr. Korn looked interested. "How's that?" he said.

Amy explained how she'd overheard the candy salesman and what she and Robin had found out. When she finished the whole story she said, "So that's why we're here. To get your reaction." She stood with her pencil poised.

"Hmph!" said Mr. Korn.

Robin leaned forward. "Is that it?"

Mr. Korn shook his head. "It only proves my point. The world's full of liars and cheats." He stalked over to the cash register.

Amy was speechless. Is that what he thought? No wonder he didn't like kids. He didn't like *anybody!* That's when Amy began to have her great revelation. It started to dawn on her that maybe some things were just meant to stay the way they were. Maybe the sign in Mr. Korn's window would never come down. Maybe it would. But what *she* needed to do, right now, was to stop worrying about it.

"Go on," Mr. Korn said. "Shoo."

Amy and Robin turned to leave. Suddenly, though, Amy stopped. "Wait," she said. "Before we go, I have something to say." She took a deep breath. "Mr. Korn, you're entitled to your opinion about people but I want you to know that I disagree. I think most people are honest and they care a lot about each other. It just depends on how you want to look at things." Then, with her head held

111

high, she said to Robin, "Come on. We're finished here."

Robin didn't say much on the way back to the treehouse. As they turned into Amy's driveway, though, she suddenly blurted, "I have something to tell you. It's about John."

Amy stopped walking.

"He wasn't driving. His girlfriend was. He lied to the police because she didn't have her license yet and he didn't want her to get into trouble."

"How do you know?" said Amy.

"When I went to talk to Mr. Whitman at the school paper, he said it was unlikely that someone with a reckless driving conviction could get a job as a schoolbus driver. He told me I had to do more research. He sent me to find Miss Eareckson, who had been John's homeroom teacher."

"And?"

"She told me that after the paper printed its story, John's girlfriend made him tell the truth. The charges against him were dropped. I guess there isn't any proof that he's a bad driver after all." She shifted from one foot to the next. "Are you mad at me?"

Amy thought about it for a minute. "No," she said finally. "It just proves what I told Mr. Korn. That most people are honest." She gave Robin a big smile. "Let's go find Leah

112

and Erin. We've still got lots of work to do if we want to get our story printed on time."

Leah and Erin were back at the treehouse, putting away the posters. "Hi, guys," Amy said, popping her head inside. "Guess who's here?" Robin's head appeared next to hers.

Leah and Erin stopped what they were doing.

"I thought you quit," said Erin.

"She changed her mind," Amy cut in.

Erin frowned. "What about John?"

Robin said in a tiny voice, "I changed my mind about that, too." She stared at the floor. "He's not so bad."

"Robin and I had the most amazing thing happen," Amy interrupted. She explained the whole story about the candy salesman.

When she'd finished, Erin said, "Wow. What did the guy say when you called him back? Was he mad we decided to write the story?"

"Oops," said Robin. "We forgot. I'll go call him right now."

"You can use our phone," Amy said. She handed Robin a pen. "Don't forget to write down his reaction. Just say, 'Any comments?' "

"I know, I know," said Robin, disappearing down the ladder.

113

Amy waited until Robin was out of earshot and said, "Is it okay with you guys that she's back?"

Erin softly kicked at the floor with her foot. "As long as she doesn't try to do everything her way."

"She won't," said Amy. "I promise. Leah?"

"It's okay with me."

"Good," said Amy. "I knew you guys would understand." She started to tell them how Robin had quit cheerleading, but decided to let Robin break the news. Instead, she crossed over to the desk and found a sheet of blank paper. "Leah, do you think you can fix the front page so our new story can be the lead?"

"Probably," she answered.

Amy sat down at the typewriter. "I'm going to start writing."

"I'll help Leah," said Erin.

Everyone worked quietly for a few minutes until the peace was interrupted by, "You guuuys. I'm back!"

"Spare me," Leah said with a groan as Chelsea burst into the treehouse. She still had on her beret.

"Hi, guys. What are you doing?" Chelsea said.

"What does it look like?" said Leah. "Working."

114

Chelsea gave a little laugh which came out sounding more like a snort. "Good thing none of you came to Roddy's house. It was really stupid."

"How come?" said Amy.

"Because Crusher never did anything except sleep. We waited for almost an hour. Roddy kept poking Crusher to get him to wake up while the mouse huddled in the other corner. Finally, a few kids started to complain so Roddy picked the poor little mouse up by the tail and dangled it in Crusher's face. That's when everyone started feeling sorry for the mouse and a bunch of kids left. Pretty soon after that Roddy's grandmother came in and made him take the mouse out. She said from now on the snake could only eat dead things."

At that moment, Robin reappeared. "Boy, was that guy mad," she said, bursting into the room. "He said the S word, the D word and the H word." She stopped when she saw Chelsea. "What are you doing here?"

"I thought you quit," Chelsea said.

"I'm back," said Robin.

"For good," added Leah.

Chelsea started chewing on a strand of her hair. "Oh." She stared around the room. "Does anyone need help?"

"No," said Leah.

115

"Oh," said Chelsea a second time. "What time is it?"

"Five o'clock," said Amy.

"I just remembered," she said. "I have to go do something." She slipped back down the ladder and hurried off.

"So much for Chelsea," said Robin.

"She'll be back," said Erin.

It was a clear, bright day one week later. In the back corner of Aegean Pizza, a party was going on. On one side of the long table sat Leah, Erin, Robin, and Amy. On the other sat Vicky, Kay, and Mr. Petropoulus. Mr. Petropoulus raised his soda can. "A toast," he said. "To my favorite newspaper reporters!"

"Cheers!" everyone answered in unison.

Amy raised her soda one more time. "And a toast to our new official advisor, Vicky."

"Thank you, thank you," said Vicky, standing up to take a little bow. "I'm honored to be associated with such a fine, upstanding newspaper."

Amy smiled modestly. She was glad everyone had liked her idea of asking Vicky to be their advisor. Amy thought it made them look more professional, and besides, Vicky *did* give good advice.

"Who wants more pizza?" said Mr. Petropoulus. "Everything's on me today."

116

Kay waved her fork. "And don't forget. Banana splits at my place when we're done here."

Amy held up her hands. "I'm stuffed. I already had three slices."

"Me too," said Robin, reaching for another.

Mr. Petropoulus shrugged. "Three, four. Who's counting?" He pointed to Amy and Robin's story. "This is worth ten slices!"

Amy grinned happily. Getting the story out on time had been a lot of extra work, but it was worth it. Mr. Petropoulus had told her that after the paper came out Mr. Capiello had called them to apologize. He'd offered to pay for all the extra cases they'd had to buy. "I told him okay and to send Walter to another route," said Mr. Petropoulus. "Maybe Siberia."

Mr. Petropoulus opened the paper to the Letters to the Editor column. "How do you like this?" he said, pointing to Mr. Korn's letter about why he didn't allow kids in his store. "That Henry is some classy guy, huh?"

"He wrote that a few weeks ago," Amy said. "Before we found out about the candy distributor."

Kay shook her head. "You'd think he'd be glad you saved him some money."

Amy shrugged. "It's not important."

Mr. Petropoulus leaned down. "Miss Pulit-

117

zer, I happen to know that is baloney. But you know what? You're right. It's not worth worrying about. You can't change what you can't change."

Amy poked at her pizza crust.

"Who's ready for banana splits?" said Kay.

"Me," said Robin and Erin in unison.

Mr. Petropoulus took off his apron and laid it across the chair. "Let's go, ladies," he said. "This is the first time in fourteen years that Kay has offered me a free banana split."

"Oh, George," said Kay with a laugh. "You know that's not true!"

Several weeks passed, and Amy had almost forgotten about the sign in Mr. Korn's window. Then one cloudy Saturday as she was on her way to deliver the latest edition of the paper, she happened to walk past the drugstore.

At first she didn't notice anything different. She was already at the end of the block, in fact, when something made her go back and check the window again. And there in the spot where the sign had once stood, a new one had taken its place. "Sale on ballpoint pens," it said. "Buy 2, get 1 free."

Amy stood there quietly, not sure whether to be happy or sad. Had the sign been taken down because Mr. Korn changed his mind or because he needed the room for another sign? It felt funny to see something she'd fought so hard for replaced by such an unimportant message.

Just then Mr. Korn put his head out the door. "I'll take some of those," he said, pointing to her newspapers.

Amy gave him a startled look. "What for?" she said, clutching them to her chest.

"My customers might want them," said Mr. Korn. "I'll leave a stack of 'em up by the cash register."

Amy's mouth fell open. "But . . ."

"Yes or no?" said Mr. Korn. "I haven't got all day."

Still in a state of shock, Amy handed him the papers. "Thanks," she said. "I, uh, appreciate this very much, Mr. Korn."

"Hmph," he answered, disappearing into the store.

Amy stood still for another minute until suddenly a huge smile crossed her face. "Yahoo," she yelled, jumping three feet into the air. "We did it! We did it!" She raced down the block, heading straight for the treehouse. "Erin, Leah, Robin," she called as she ran. "Wait until you hear what happened. You aren't going to believe it! Mr. Korn has finally changed his mind!"

Readers:

Win an authentic

TREEHOUSE TIMES TOTE-PACK

1000 Lucky Winners chosen at random will receive our attractive navy, white and green over-the-shoulder tote.

To Enter:

Fill in the coupon below or print your name, address, age and phone number on a 3 x 5 card and mail either to:

THE TREEHOUSE TIMES

TOTE-PACK DRAWING

c/o AVON BOOKS   Box 789   Dresden, TN 38225

Winners will be chosen in a random drawing by the representatives of AVON BOOKS on November 15th. Winners will be alerted and receive their totes within 6 weeks of that date. Some entrants will receive a consolation prize in lieu of tote, while supplies last. For a list of winners, please supply a self-addressed stamped envelope with entry. No other correspondence regarding this drawing will be undertaken.

No purchase necessary. Offer available on displays for THE TREEHOUSE TIMES in some stores. VOID WHERE PROHIBITED.

NAME_____AGE_____

ADDRESS_____

_____ ZIP_____

Where did you buy this book?

_____

GOOD LUCK!